CLARE FISH   rea-
tive Writin   re
the author   ng,
2017), and th   *Gets
In (Influx Press, 2010). Then work has ... shed
internationally, won a Betty Trask Award and been
longlisted for the Edgehill Short Story Award and the
International Dylan Thomas Prize. They live in Leeds.

CLARE FISHER

THE
MOON IS
TRENDING

SALT
MODERN
STORIES

SALT

CROMER

PUBLISHED BY SALT PUBLISHING 2023

2 4 6 8 10 9 7 5 3 1

First published in Great Britain in 2023 by
Salt Publishing Ltd
12 Norwich Road, Cromer, Norfolk NR27 0AX United Kingdom

www.saltpublishing.com

Salt Publishing Limited Reg. No. 5293401

A CIP catalogue record for this book is available from the British Library

ISBN 978 1 78463 287 8 (Paperback edition)
ISBN 978 1 78463 288 5 (Electronic edition)

Typeset in Granjon by Salt Publishing

Printed and bound in Great Britain by Clays Ltd, St Ives plc

Contents

WTAF

T HE MOON IS trending. There is a spider crawling across Sophia's forehead, it is a very small spider; in fact, I'm not sure if it is or isn't a spider, but it is, nevertheless, a creature that she will not want anywhere near her body; she will probably yell at me for not telling her sooner, which I could only do if I were to interrupt her story about her friend's boyfriend and how he sets timers at three-hour intervals throughout the night so that he can 'feed' his avatar in some computer game to which he is unhealthily attached; he hasn't left their flat in months and there is a constant crust at the corners of his eyes, as if he is constantly waking up, Sophie says that her friend says, but if she were to turn off his alarms, he would cry; the friend knows this even though she has never seen him cry, she has never seen any man cry, she is not sure men can cry, which she knows is a cliché, but hey, clichés exist for a reason. The spider is now on Sophia's cheek, and the boyfriend, he has actually stopped going to work, he expects Sophia's friend to pay his rent as well as cook and clean and fetch the gaming paraphernalia he keeps ordering from her—well, it's actually her Dad's—Amazon, and every now and then, she thinks: this can't go on, which is exactly what I am thinking re Sophia's attachment to her friend's boyfriend's attachment to his computer-game avatar; she tells me it almost every time we meet, and even when she tells me other things, e.g. the moon is trending, she is telling me it; she is telling me it when she tells me that on the way home for work, she saw this massive queue outside this massive warehouse, she thought it was for something really exciting and she felt annoyed that all the people in the queue knew about it and she didn't, so she joined it, and after what felt like forever but was probably about six minutes, she asked the woman in front what they were all waiting for, and the woman looked at her like she'd said something very rude and she whispered something to the child who Sophia had only just noticed was standing beside her, and the child asked what she'd asked, and she told them, and the child said nothing for what felt like another *ever*, and then they said, it's for food, and then she said, oh, and she turned and she moved away from the queue as quickly as she could without running; she didn't want them to think that she hated them, it was more that she hated herself, or something, and the moon is trending, the moon is trending, although how, exactly, can the moon be trending, does it have a twitter account and who on earth runs it, wh—*what*

The actual.

Fuck?

She slaps her cheek. *Was there something on my face?* Her eyebrows crease at an accusatory angle.

No.

I felt something. She slaps it again. *I definitely felt*

something. *But you'd tell me, wouldn't you?*

Of course, I say, and how I feel is like I've snorted a glass of Prosecco, which is how Sophia says her friend says she feels when her boyfriend turns the volume of his console down so low that she hopes, for a second or sometimes two, that it's off.

No Sense of Direction

THE GIRL WAS absolutely not going to look at her
phone because   mindfulness
   because the last time she looked at it, which was literally
just now, it said that the distance between the bobbing blue
dot that was (not) her body and the hipster tap room that
would soon or might already contain the Boy (who might
just be The One)'s body (which she imagined as a bobbing
blue dot, even though it wouldn't show as one on *her* phone,
only his, though maybe, if he did turn out to be The One,
they'd find an app that would change this) was a 1.78 km
straight line along the canal tow path that she was now on
because *focus*
   because looking at her phone was only gonna slow time
down to a dribble and not a generic dribble but the dribble
that dribbled out of her night-mouth in such quantities
such that she frequently awoke with an entirely wet pillow,
which was the last thing she should be thinking about on
her way to meet the Boy (that might just be The One),
surely.

What her phone didn't know, not even in satellite mode,

was about the dog shit; how it was dangling from the bald branches of the bushes that lined the towpath. Some psycho's idea of a Christmas decoration! Maybe she would tell the Boy (her Best Friend would tell her off for thinking he might be The One but who she couldn't help thinking might be The One; yes, they'd only talked via Tinder chat, which was less intimate, somehow, than WhatsApp, but there was a Vibe, there defo was) all about it. Maybe it would make walking this straight line seem dangerous and exciting. Maybe it would make *her* seem dangerous and exciting! But—wait.

Wait.

Dog shit.

Dog shit?

Dog shit in plastic bags dangling from branches?

Dog shit and psychos?

On a first date? Was she mental? Best Friend would by now be wiping laughter-tears from her eyes and whilst she did so, she'd be looking at Girl's body in that way that made her feel certain that if she were to look at her phone, the blue dot would have exploded all over her Maps, which of course it hadn't, and of course, she should not be thinking about it because thinking about your phone was halfway to looking at it, which is what she was now doing, bloody hell, did she have no self-control!? Evidently not, but that was not the sort of self-talk the sort of Insta accounts she'd never admit to Best Friend that she followed would tell her to use, though it was possible, given there was no way to make your followers secret, that Best Friend already knew; she might, as Girl shortened what now felt like more of a wiggly gravel smudge than a straight line, be lying on her bed and scrolling through Girl's followers, which was a thing Girl often—

But no.

No message from Best Friend to see how it was going.

No message from Boy saying he was excited; no words to confirm her suspicion (that was really an intuition, that those Insta accounts said was the only *real* real) that the increasing density of emojis in his last few messages meant that he, too, was trying not to wonder whether she was his One.

No new Tinder Likes.

No new Reactions to her Story about failing to water her plants.

No other notifications, not even from Facebook, not even the sort of notifications that aren't notifications, e.g. that some girl you don't even remember friending is 'interested' in a macrame workshop in Cardiff, even though she lives in Newcastle.

When she looked up from the screen there was somehow less to look at than before. As if all those not-notifications had gobbled up part of the sky. The platform trainers Best Friend had

insisted made her look like a spaceman slash Spice Girl were now caked with mud; and in the bright artificial H&M lights Girl had believed it, but now, now, with no one to look at her, not even the geese, who were more interested in whatever goop or fish were living under the water, she felt like a hippo like a weirdo like some 'o' too weird to name.

Why wasn't she there yet? No more poo bags; no bars, either. The blue Google Maps dot, the one usually throbbing wherever she stood, was still at that awkward cross-roads outside the station. And it did not throb. Had it died? Dots didn't die, stupid! Stupido hippo weirdo psycho arrghh oooohhh! What even was she?

Late. That's what. Or was it a where? Boy was probably worrying she'd stood him up. Probably attaching various 'o's to her name. But she couldn't even message him—the app wouldn't load.

Fuck.

No one around, so she said it out loud.

Fuck. Fuckfuckfuck.

FUCK.

F U   C   K.

She skimmed her fucks across the water.

It made her feel the sort of good that did not depend on someone else watching, maybe because she was watching herself almost as if she was someone else, or two people— one the one she'd known her whole life, one she'd never met, despite being, like, twenty-two, which was probably too old to be thinking of herself as a Girl, but *woman* sounded much too serious and she didn't take herself too seriously, but not to the extent that she would put that sort of thing on her dating profile: that was one of the things they'd bonded over, her and Boy, and how much they hated the sort of people who were too stupid to realise that doing that sort of thing was a sign, ironically enough, of how seriously they took themselves.

At last! A turning. This had to be it.

But no.

No.

She was now at The Windmill, which was not the

hipster tap room where the boy had probably had just about enough of waiting, maybe he was downing his pint of what he'd claimed was the best real ale in the whole region, she didn't like real ale, or fake ale, though she'd not told him that, so maybe he'd bought her a pint that he was now having to down; maybe he was running outside to throw up, or to burp massively, though boys never ran anywhere to burp, they just let their bodies burp or do whatever they wanted, wherever.

The journey from the station to The Windmill was a zigzag, and The Windmill was nowhere near the canal, it was literally at the top of a hill, and so how had she got here? Maybe she had actually agreed to meet Boy here? Maybe the tap room was disguising itself as The Windmill? Yes, maybe it was an April Fool's (in September).

When she walked in, an old man stared at her. She stared back at him, focussing on his chin dimple, which was so well-defined, she wondered whether he'd done it with a pencil. Then he resumed staring at the television screen that all of the other men, a lot of whom weren't even that old, were staring at, and she was glad; she was almost getting into this whole not-being-looked at thing.

There was no TV in the back room; no men, either: just grubby velvet chairs and a truly terrible painting of a horse galloping towards some clouds containing a golden gate that may or may represent heaven, and—

Best Friend.

She was there. Which was almost Girl's here.

She clearly believed herself to be eating a sandwich whilst reading a book when what she was actually doing was holding the book half-open with her left hand, which was stuck in a painful-looking claw, whilst staring at her right hand as if this would magically stop the slices of mayo-slathered tomato falling into the gap between the pages of the book that her claw was just about holding open, which of course it didn't (this wasn't that dumb Netflix series where the teen girl who looked like a lesbo but, like all the other TV girls and women who were not psychos, fell in love with the guy who basically stalked her for several episodes, could make things move or blow up or shrink or triple in size just by looking at them, which they both agreed was pretty cool even though they also agreed the show was totally babyish and dumb, and they'd never tell anyone else that they'd watched it not once but twice, the second time in lieu of going to a house party, and in only their pants and strap tops) and so the tomato slopped all over the pages but did Best Friend admit defeat? No, she did not, she *was* Best Friend after all; she just dropped the sandwich back onto the plate and tightened her claw and wiped the tomato off the paper with her finger and then put it all (finger, tomato, mayo, and probably some microscopic particles of paper and ink) into her mouth and closed her eyes and smiled as if she knew perfectly well that a more accurate way of describing her current situation was reading a sandwich whilst eating a book and that this, moreover, was exactly what s—

    t ripped.

Yes, in some pocket of time that refused to fit into any sentence, Girl had tripped. And now was spread all over the carpet like a spaceman trying to be a Spice Girl trying to be a starfish.

How did you get here?

I don't know. She tried to explain about the lines and the dots and the shit bags, but when Best Friend's book thudded against her foot, she stopped.

Best Friend's mouth twitched at the corners, like she was trying not to laugh. *You're actually interrupting my* date.

Oh god! Sorry! With who? Is he in the toilet? Though he's been gone a long time . . . Does he have IBS?

No. Best Friend play-slapped Girl's hand. *With myself.*

With yourself!

Yeah.

And is it going well?

Better than expected.

Then Best Friend's finger was in her mouth. It had been in her mouth for some time—longer than the time it would take to suck the sauce off it. Girl moved around the table and sat right next to Best Friend. Their shoulders bumped. She grabbed Best Friend's hand and pulled it until it popped. Then it was as if all the versions of them that had been skulking in different corners of the room rushed together, and their lips rushed towards each other's lips, and even though it wasn't the sort of thing Girl had ever thought about doing because she wasn't gay and neither was Best Friend, they'd both been dating guys for as long as they'd been friends, and yes sometimes she did think about Best Friend's and various other friends' shoulders bums hips boobs smiles when she was fucking the boys who she fucked but that wasn't exactly thinking, and how could be she be gay if she was fucking boys; but how her lips felt when Best Friend was kissing them was like they were the lips of the boy whose body was the only place this line could possibly end.

Where's Your Head At?

NOBODY KNEW WHERE they came from, not even the internet.

One moment, the air between the walls and the furniture and the people was filled with nothing besides dust, water droplets, thoughts of things people wanted to do to other people but would never dare, thoughts of things people did not want to buy but wanted to think about more than they did the things they did not really believe they had ever done to other people, and other things so small that they looked like nothing; the next, it was filled with furry headless bats.

The bats were the size of over-fed domestic cats. They flapped their wings with a frenzy that was at once terrifying, pitiful and hilarious. At first, everybody thought they were a dream that was probably also a nightmare. Nobody knew that this same thought was in the body of every other body in the country, almost like a virus.

Of course, the air quickly filled with words that attempted to untangle the truth of the bats. The words flapped and flailed between bodies in much the same way that the bats were still flapping and flailing between walls and objects, and even after approximately 29183957172948 of them had been shared online (although 29184 of them were repetitions of the same seven memes), everybody still believed, in the place that would never make it out of their bodies or into the internet, that they were in a dream; yes, this was really happening; yet it was also impossible.

Some people clubbed the bats with the other sort of bat. Other people sprayed them with poison. Richer people paid poorer people to club or poison their indoor bats; outdoor bats, they shot for fun. The clubbing and the spraying filed time to an arrow that pointed, ever so elegantly, towards a batless future in which nobody would ever complain about anything else ever again. This future lasted no more than five hours, during which everyone lay about in a stunned silence, not daring to see what lurked in each other's eyes, nor even in those of memes and gifs, which of course did not really have eyes, only to resume, by the sixth or seventh hour, their complaints re those aspects of their lives that were unrelated to the absence or presence of bats, such as their sofa, and how it was too wide in a way that felt very narrow. By the twelfth hour, the air between the walls and the furniture and the people between the walls and the furniture was so thick with complaining, that when the bats reappeared, everyone was relieved. They immediately uploaded photos of the new bats to the internet, accompanied by all manner of complain-adjacent emojis. *Can't believe the little fuckers are back again. This time we'll beat them once and for all. Oh, yeah!*

But there was a significant minority of people who did not club or spray their bats. However, because not clubbing or spraying the bats was now a criminal offence—those who'd been caught were blamed for the bats' continued existence, even though the ones who did the blaming knew, also, that the clubbing and the spraying only discontinued them temporarily—so these people did not tell any other people that they were *this* sort of person, not inside, not outside, not even on the internet. These people just lived with the bats. Some did this by flapping at any bat that was in their way; the more accurately they mimicked the bats' movement, the more space they cleared between their bodies and the bats' bodies. Others constructed special wafters; these they propped by the door of every room in their house. Others did nothing to postpone the moment when their bodies and the bats' bodies collided; the bats flew into their foreheads, and they did not die, they did not contract any of the 291835 diseases that the internet claimed that physical contact with the bats would cause: the bats' fur tickled their noses; many sneezed.

A few began to look forward to such collisions, or even to move in ways that they hoped would make the collisions happen. The bats, however, despite their headlessness—which still no one had explained—sensed when a person was trying to force a collision, and if, as occasionally happened, a human, in an effort to stretch out the collision into something like a relationship, attempted to clasp the bats' delightfully soft and furry bodies to their chests, the bats screamed a scream so horrendous, the offending person would let go *immediately*. The bats did what the bats did and no human could stop them from doing it; this was a truth the non-clubbing non-spraying people learned over the course of many screams. If they were lucky enough to touch those bodies that were so like yet unlike human bodies, they did their best to not-hear the place in their chest that wanted more more *more*, amplifying, instead, the part that understood *enough*. When these people came into contact with other people who were in this significant minority, they did not think: we are the same sorts of people. They thought: these other people are unbearably smug.

Leak-Proof

T HERE WAS SOMETHING wrong with our swimming
pool and I knew it and Dad knew it and Mum knew
it and Jess knew it and we all knew that we all knew it but
no one was saying it, and if we went on not-saying it much
longer, I'd explode.

I tried to say it whilst Dad was driving me to swim practice. The words scraped the backs of my braces, desperate
to leave the home they'd outgrown, but when I opened
my mouth, out came the sentence: *Isn't it sad about Trishy
Brownfield?*

Dad made a face at the roundabout. *You always used to
cover your ears when I put on her records.*

*So? That doesn't mean I want her to die in a pool of her
own—*

*—How did you hear about that? Have you been spending
too much time on the internet?*

—We all spend too much time on the internet.

By now, we'd stopped in the leisure centre car park and
he was reaching for his phone.

—What?

I didn't really care about Trishy Brownfield; neither did

most of the internet people who said they did. The problem was, I'd read so much about how much other people cared about it, it was almost as if I did.

I pulled at the door but it was child-locked. *Dad?*

He grabbed my hand. *I'm sorry I couldn't build you a pool big enough to properly practise in.* He was looking into my eyes. He was looking into my eyes even though he never looked into anyone's eyes, and how it made me feel was like a prawn that was about to be peeled. *But it's better than nothing, no? And it's still good fun, all splashing around together?*

Yes, Dad. It is.

All I ever wanted, growing up, was a pool. A pool of my own.

I know. He'd been saying this one to four times a week for years and years.

There was lots we didn't have, lots of things most people would say were more necessary than a pool, but it was a pool I missed. I wanted somewhere to just . . . float.

Coach Laska is going to make angry eyebrows at me again.

But after two or three seconds of floating, he went on, as if I hadn't spoken, *I bash into the side. Mind you, you're a lot small —*

Open the door.

But—

—Dad!

He hung his head. *Sorry.*

The warmup was almost over by the time I slid into the water. Coach Laska's eyebrows burrowed towards her nose: *how is it you have parents to drive you everywhere and do everything for you and you're still late?* Then her mouth told me to do twelve lengths of front crawl. I nodded. But I did backstroke. I kept on doing backstroke after she shouted at me for doing it.

◊

What was wrong with our swimming pool was that no matter how many gallons of water Dad pumped into it, it refused to stay full. At first, it stayed at the three-quarter mark. Mum said it was stylish, showing off the pretty tiles round the side. Now, though, six months since we'd installed it, it was closer to half-full; when Dad flopped onto the lilo, he crashed right down to the concrete bottom, pushing even more water out and onto Mum's new dress. She said the sort of nothing that made even me doubt whether what had just happened had actually just happened. (She's like that with her *nothings*, my mum).

Every few days, he'd wake us up by rubbing our damp swimming costumes in our faces, then making us hunt for treasure before breakfast. By *treasure* he meant mouldy pennies. By *hunt*, he meant shiver and kick and dive, whilst he watched, en-fleeced, from the side. I let Jess catch it every time, though it took her a while to notice:

—*You're not even trying.*

—*I hate this game.*

Dad flinched.

—*You used to love it.*

—*Yeah, and people change. Anyway, it's no fun in a pool this shallow.* My words opened a window I didn't know was in the air, and fresher air rushed through it—or maybe it was just the breeze.

—And I'm freezing. We live in Yorkshire, not California! And, and, and—my head was sticking out of the window, I was about to fall out, I was about to fall out and tumble to my death and I couldn't wait—*our pool has a leak.*

—Pip. Dad said my name as if he was in charge of all the world's words and he had decided that it was the stupidest. *This pool is leak-proof.*

Waterproof jackets don't stay waterproof forever. The rain gets in and your skin gets all—

—but the whole point of a pool, Dad interrupted, *is to keep the water in, not out! And is there or is there not water in there?*

Yes, but—

He jumped into the pool; the water level rose an inch.—*See!*

Then Jess started to shiver, the clouds started to rain, Mum said she'd make us pancakes, and we spent the rest of the day eating them whilst watching this TV show set in California—a show I used to like, but which now made me feel as if that window I'd, with much effort, opened, was slamming shut.

When the water got so low that you could barely swim without your belly scraping the floor, Mum started her morning constitutionals. She went so early that no one saw her doing it; all we'd see, when we came down for breakfast, was her wet hair, her wet swimming costume, and the way her eyes shone as she said things like: *it injects a va-va-voom into my day,* and: *it's like squirting Fairy Liquid right into your soul.*

—Pip, why don't you follow your mother's example? Get some extra practice in?

—*Give the girl a break! She does enough practise as it is. The home pool is the fun pool.*

—*No one else at school has a swimming pool*, Jess piped up.

—*Yes, and you should remember how lucky you are. And never to show off.*

—*They don't believe me. They said our garden's not big enough for a pool.*

—*What?* Dad craned his neck towards the window, as if to check. There wasn't really much of a garden left; just the patio, a thin border of grass, and the pool. I didn't know who in Jess's class had said this, but I already knew we'd get along. *Invite them round.*

—*Invite your whole class round! Have a pool party!*

—*Yes, a pool party. Good idea, very good. Pip, you invite people, too. Invite your swim team!*

Three weeks later, we had a pool party. Jess invited her entire class; I invited no one. The morning of the party was sunny, and Mum was up early making sandwiches that she claimed were shaped like sharks but which looked more like sperm. Dad waded around the remaining four inches of water, saying that if he could travel back in time and tell his twelve-year-old self that his twelve-year-old daughter was about to have a pool party, his twelve-year-old self would cry even though crying wasn't a thing that his twelve-year-old self was ever allowed to do, his brothers had made sure of that, ha ha, and that was why he'd never told them about the pool or anything; in fact, the first person he told was Mum, and she did not laugh, did not pretend to be sympathetic, only to then viciously superglue his pants to his bum, did not in any way punish him for it, and that was how he knew she was a keeper.

—*Aw, isn't he cute?*

Mum and Dad wrinkled their noses at each other.

Then the doorbell rang. It rang and rang again. A cloud appeared, then disappeared. The space around the pool filled with goosepimply arms and legs.

—*Jump in! Enjoy yourselves!*

—*You won't believe how fun it is!*

Then a little boy whose name I still don't know—he's not been invited again—stammered: *it's not a pool, it's just an empty hole in the ground.*

The window was wide open and the wind that blew through it was very cold, very strong. I could no longer feel my fingers or my toes. I could, however, feel something else, I didn't know what.

—*It's still a pool,* said a girl with a swimming costume with two frills running down its middle which flapped and flapped in the wind. *It just doesn't have water in it.*

—*Of course it's a pool,* said Mum, shaking her head. *This is a* pool party!

Then she and Dad laughed in that too-loud way that scratched my spine. I tried to catch Jess's eye but she was frowning at the teeny-tiny black drain in the pool's now-exposed bottom, as if willing it to suddenly burp back up all the water it had swallowed.

—*And this, I'll have you know*, said Dad, *is the best pool within a seventeen-mile radius.*

—*A* radius? Yelled the girl. There were, I noticed, two black dots just above her costume's frills, though I couldn't work out what they were for. *That's the circumference divided by two times pi and I don't mean two eating pies, silly,* she paused, laughing as if she could barely believe she'd told such a funny joke, *I mean the one with no e and you can't eat it because it's maths and it looks like a table.*

—*That's lovely maths, dear,* said Mum. *I bet you can do some lovely swimming, too?*

The girl gripped one of her frills, then let it go. *I'm a platinum dolphin already.*

—*In that case,* said Dad, *why don't you show us what you can do?*

—*Yeah,* jeered someone from the back, *show us why you're a swimming boffin.*

Then Mum and Dad began to clap. The other kids joined on. The girl frowned at the concrete, looked at Mum, but Mum nodded and smiled, and then she bent her little legs, shut her eyes, held her nose, and jumped.

I'm not sure what was worse: the sound of her knees hitting the dry white tiles, the silence that followed the sound, the howl that followed the silence, or how it was only when she began to writhe and wriggle with pain that I understood: her costume's frills and dots were meant to represent the wings and the eyes of a bird, probably an owl.

Parents were summoned. In the gap between the front of our house and the front of the cars, there was talk of ambulances and law suits and responsibility.

—*I don't know what all the fuss is about,* Dad said, seven hours later, which was how long it took us, running back and forth with kettles and buckets and hoses, to fill the pool back up. *She should've known not to bomb.* It was dark by this point; dark, with a wind whose bite felt somehow personal. But Dad got into the water, then Mum, then

Jess, and—because the impossible window was, despite the wind, locked shut—me.

—*Nothing makes you feel alive like jumping into cold water!* said Dad.

For once, I had to agree. I agreed so much that when we went back inside, Mum's sandwiches looked a bit more like sharks.

The next morning, however, the pool was emptier than empty. Mum looked at it the way people on the internet said they felt when they'd first looked at that photo of that man looking at Trishy Brownfield's body floating in that pool in that part of the world that had the climate for pools.

—*No morning constitutional?* Dad asked.

—*I . . . Do you think we should get someone to come and look at it . . . just in case?*

The silence that followed was a close relation of the one that had followed the girl's bomb: an aunt, maybe even a sibling.

—*There's nothing wrong with it.*

—*No, of course not.*

Dad ran outside, turned on the tap, ran back inside.— *I'll call them anyway. Just in case.*

By the time the technician arrived, the pool was burping water all over the grass, Mum and Dad were beaming, but I—I wished I'd spent longer looking at it when it was emptier than empty.

—*You've overfilled it.* The man made the sort of face that was meant to make Dad feel like an idiot; he had no way of knowing that Dad was incapable of seeing himself as anything less than a genius.

—*He only did that because the water keeps draining out of it,* said Jess.

—*That's not what happened,* said Dad. He folded his arms at the technician. *This is just how I like it. Full.*

—*So is there a leak or isn't there a leak?*

—*This model is leak-proof.*

—*Leak proof doesn't mean leaks don't occur.*

—*It isn't leaking.*

—*So why did you call me?*

—*Can you just check whether there is a possibility that it might, one day, in the distant future, be leaking?*

The technician looked, then, at me. I felt as if he saw what I saw. Or as if he saw that I didn't see what the rest of my family saw. It was a good feeling. An open-window feeling.

—*Sure.*

Smiling at me, he did with the control panel whatever it is technicians do with control panels. Then he said that there were no leaks or any other problems that he could see.

Dad nodded.—*That's exactly what I thought.*

—*The pool's empty again.* I had to shout it two or three times before Mum and Dad heard; they were watching *The Little Mermaid* on the max volume, just like they'd done the night before and the night before and the night before that, and for however long it had been—maybe months, maybe hours; the pool made time feel all flubbery and wrong—since the water had disappeared to wherever it disappeared to.

—*Stop being so negative*, Mum snapped.

—*I'm just saying what's there.*

—*No, you're saying what's not there. You're saying the glass is half empty*—

—*It's not half empty, it's completely empty.*

—*What's empty?* Dad's swimming trunks squelched between his legs. He'd come from upstairs; he must've wetted them in the shower.

—*Pip's silly brain,* giggled Jess.

—*Yes,* said Dad. *I did wonder what was going on with your sister. You know, Coach Laska called me last week . . . She said she won't listen to instructions, she does the wrong stroke, or sometimes, she refuses to swim at all.*

Mum looked me a long, hard nothing. Then she looked at the pool. *Maybe we should get that technician back.* A smile pulled her lips apart; on her front right tooth, I spied a herb. *One more time. Just in case.*

The technician's lips quivered as if he was making a huge and continuous effort not to laugh.—*Why don't you show me how you're filling it?* he said to Dad.

—*It's a very simple mechanism and I am a trained engineer.*

—*Just show me.*

—*OK, but I assure you I'm doing it right.*

They went outside. When they returned, Dad's face was arranged in a position I'd never seen before—a position which implied he was beginning to consider the possibility that the future in which he stopped being a genius might be about now.

—*He hadn't pressed the seal button.* The technician chuckled. *Easy mistake to make. Very easy, especially as*—

—*That'll be all,* said Dad.

The technician made sure to smirk at me before he left.

There were no more problems with the pool after that. You could swim a solid four or five strokes before grazing your fingers at its edge. But Mum stopped going for her constitutionals. Dad stopped saying how great it was. We stopped talking about it and swimming in it and lounging in it, not even in the heatwave, which we spent mostly in the living room, in our underwear, with the doors shut. Coach Laska struck me off the swim team; a great loss, she said, for if I hadn't insisted on morale-destroying behaviour, such as climbing out of the pool after just half a length of a stroke, so bizarre she'd not even dare name it, then lying on the side of the pool, whale-like, and refusing to get up, I would've been a real asset. You could've won, she'd said, wiping from her eye what I am almost sure was an imaginary tear, many competitions.

I had lost something, yes, but it wasn't the swim team. I didn't know what it was, but sometimes it woke me up in the middle of the night for absolutely no reason. My heart would beat very, very fast, as if I'd been dreaming of a race, only I hadn't dreamt of any race, I hadn't dreamt at all; I had simply passed from one kind of darkness to another.

If I couldn't get back to sleep, I'd go outside and jump in the pool. I'd swim as fast as I could—not because there was any race to win, but because of the cold. When my body was numb, I'd stop. Floating on my back, I'd imagine what I'd see if I was in some place close enough to people-less to see the stars.

Sleep always came easy after that, and if it wasn't for my damp chlorine-infused pillows, I'd be sure that my excursion had been a dream.

Once or twice, at breakfast, I thought about telling Dad; about just floating in the water and how I felt like I'd dived through that impossible window once and for all. But I didn't. I just looked at the parts of the internet I wanted to look at whilst he looked at the parts of the internet he wanted to look at whilst Mum scolded us both for looking at our respective parts of the internet instead of at where our fingers were putting our toast.—*My purpose in life is not to pick up your crumbs!*

Then, one night, I slid open the patio door only to discover that it was already open. Through that neither darkness nor light that is whatever it is that happens just before dawn, I saw Dad. He was squatting in the Shallow End, the water was lapping at his neck, and he was staring at the Deep End. How he looked was like the child in his stories—the one whose pool is always trapped in the future.

In the morning, the pool was empty again, but Mum was scolding Dad for dropping crumbs as if this was the only thing worth noticing.

I slid the patio doors all the way open.

The draught! Mum yelled, but I was already bending my knees, ready to jump.

My feet left the ground, and it seemed, for a moment, like I was really going somewhere. Maybe I'd finally explode.

Well, I did not explode. I scraped the heels of my hands on the pool's concrete bottom.

—*Why are you smiling?* The child ran outside to ask me this. He was tall, with greying hair, a beer belly and a few patches of stubble.

—*Maybe we should call back that technician?* There was something in the nothing between Mum's words now: some desperate thing. *Just in case.*

—*No.* Dad was fiddling with the control panel; the child was gone, and what he'd done with it, I didn't know, didn't want to know, I did want to know, I would never know, I'd always known. *The knobs are as they should be.*

Water gurgled up from the drain between my feet.

Soon, I was squatting in a puddle.

Then, my jeans were wet.

Mum was yelling about chlorine, Jess was yelling about her school nickname, dry vadge, Mum was yelling at her to stop yelling *vadge* in the garden, Jess was yelling at Mum that in yelling at her to stop yelling vadge in the garden, she was herself was yelling vadge in the garden; Dad was yelling at them to stop yelling. I stayed in the pool, which was neither full nor empty—a perspective from which their voices looked just like the hammy smiles of the people on the TV show watched by the people in that Californian TV show, which we no longer watched.

Think Outside The Box

THE BOX—WE WERE meant to think outside of it, to
Think instead of think, to Think Things no one had
ever Thought or even thought before, but our bodies were
inside of it, so. We would wake up. Some of us would roll
over and go back to sleep and others of us would pound
our fists against the brown, brown walls and others of us
would look at the pretend-sleepers and the wall-pounders
and howl.

This did not, as the producers frequently reminded us,
make for good TV; it did not make for bad TV, neither
the kind that was good nor the kind that was bad in a way
that made watchers feel good; it was a the sort of neither
good nor bad that stopped anyone from watching, or from
even blogging or tweeting or talking about why they were
or weren't watching. 'Just imagine,' they'd say, 'you could
be suffering all this and no one would know . . . it could
all be . . . for nothing!'

Needless to say, even those of us who considered
ourselves rebellious would rather follow the producers'
orders than venture any further down the path of psychic
calamity that was their suggestion re the pointlessness of

the whole endeavour; we all tried, in the hours after each reminder, extra hard. We thought. We thought and we thought and we thought. Some of us rubbed each other's backs whilst we did so, others rubbed our foreheads against the wall. One paced whilst making a clicking noise with his tongue which he denied making and which would've driven the rest of us mad, were it not for his ability to occasionally produce, and almost at the moment that we'd given up hope, a Thought. The air would thicken; it smelt like rotting daisies, no, like fresh daisies, like rot and daisies, like daisies that began to rot before they were born, not that they'd ever been born, no one gets born inside the box, everyone knows that.

Anyway. We'd flop into a pile then roll towards the wall and push and push and push and push and just when we thought we couldn't push anymore, the wall would give, and we'd fall, someone would always elbow someone else, although who did what and to whom, we'd never know, it all happened too fast, so fast, we could never be sure what had happened at all, or if, indeed, it had happened, some reported flashes of neon, others, a sheet of rubber billowing in the wind, then someone else would say, look, there's more space, so much more, and we'd run; we'd run and run and run; and just when we were about to say what we were thinking i.e. maybe this was the outside we'd been trying to Think ourselves towards all this time, we'd hit our heads against the wall. The wall was black, no, pink, it was rainbow, rubber, crinkled foil, a patchwork of terrible cartoon dogs with eyes that never stopped googling at us.

Then would commence the Theorising, re were we In or Out, was Out another way of spelling In or ought we to combine them into some other possibility altogether, and why had it now been so long since the producers had been in contact? Could it be that we were no longer being watched that we were thinking and talking and failing to Think into the void that was everything that people are not that didn't care one way or another what we did or didn't?

Or, or, or, or—was it that we were dead? Yes, we nodded as if our skulls were mere components of a much larger, cleverer skull that could see us even if we couldn't see it, that was the most likely explanation re why they'd not been in touch. We were dead and they were watching us, and in the meaninglessness of our suffering, they saw the meaningfulness of their own. And so began the moment when all this stopped sounding true.

Living the Dream

N OT ONE OF the twenty-four angry faces would tell
me why I was in the mansion or why, even though
I was the cause of the anger, they would not let me leave.
They stood shoulder to shoulder, with their feet planted
wide and their arms folded. If they hadn't looked so serious,
and been wearing clothes that imbued the word frumpy
with several extra, itchy layers of reality, I'd have taken
them for parody gangsters. When it became clear that they
weren't going to move, I sat down on the carpet, which was
very red and very, very soft, and I closed my eyes. I dug my
fingers into the red, red soft. I began to feel that my being
there wasn't such a problem, after all. Then a smelly new
wetness appeared on my left calf. I opened my eyes. A tiny
monkey was crouched there, shitting. The shit was reddish
brown and liquid. I screamed. I stood up. Someone pushed
me back down and the monkey's claws dug right through
my jeans and my skin and now its shit was mixing with my
blood and I shook my leg but it dug harder and I jumped
up and down but it shook harder still and I must've been
screaming help because the non-gangsters were saying,
we can't, we can't, you've done this to yourself, you only

need to calm down and accept what fate is bringing to you, and the shit was now seeping inside my sock, this isn't the time for philosophy, I said, and they said that that much was obvious, and they hated philosophy, it was so removed from the realities of life, they all stared at the monkey shit when they said *life,* and by this point I was so tired, I lay down and closed my eyes and stopped trying to change myself or anything and just when I thought I had dissolved into the carpet, they started to clap. I opened my eyes. The non-gangsters were now standing in two neat rows on either side of the doorway. You're free to go. But the thought of going back into the world that was so, so much bigger than this mansion, and contained so, so, so many more disgusting and frumpy creatures, was no longer so appealing. Sure, I said, but could I first have a shower?

Of course, it was one of those rainforest ones which destroy ten miles of the Amazon with every use. It was glorious.

Stophanie

S TEPHANIE, OR 'STOP-HANIE', as, thanks to a meme made by an assistant garage attendant in Wisconsin, US, she is now known, Grapper was en route from her office to one of the many retail outlets in MoreCityProductivityPark, when she just—stopped. She is, as you no doubt, unless you live under a wifi-4g-5g-less stone, all know, still stopped. Security tried to remove her; bosses threatened to fire her; bosses did fire her; security threatened the police, the police threatened fines, the police gave out fines, then called the fire department, who still could not move her, and there isn't a scientist in the world who can explain why even the country's strongest and most expensive crane, one which has knocked down not one but three and a half twenty-seven storey buildings, failed to move her. Are we at WholeTruth Productions satisfied with this? No, we are not. We are, in the words of our founder, Ferg Mint, guided 'by the truth of our own eyes and our own eyes only.' And whilst that Wisconsin garage attendant is now making memes about that cat whose farts sound like the solutions to impossible maths equations, we have gathered as much truth as was witnessed by eyes of those at the scene of the crime, no, it's not a crime, the act, as possible, and whilst we aren't so arrogant as to say *it's the 'whole', we'll say that it's not far off. It's not far at all.*

TK, Trainee Security Guard, FlipFlop Pharmacy

If you watch the video footage, you'll see her walking towards Don't-Nuts, and then, about three and a half floor squares away from it, she just – stops. People walk around her. A kid scoots around her. Then a man carrying a tray of coffees whilst staring at his phone bashes into her. He waves his hands at the brown that is now spreading all down his chinos and onto the tiles; there is a fire in his eyes, like, he's so angry, but he's happy that, at last, he can pin all his life's problems, of which the brown is somehow symbolic, on this one cause.

Garry says that it's impossible to see things like this. That if I didn't spend so much time trying, nevertheless, to see them, I'd have graduated from Trainee to Assistant Security Guard. He says that if I had, in this instance, focused on what was *in front* of me, I might have stopped her before she'd stopped. When I pointed out that she wasn't committing a crime, and that even if she had, I'd have not been permitted to do anything, given that she was more than two floor tiles away from FlipFlop's doors – I thought about mentioning that kid he didn't stop stabbing the other kid for the same reason, then changed my mind – he told me to stop making excuses for myself.

Garry sees women in terms of whether or not he'd fuck them; men, in terms of whether he'd beat them at a fight. I don't know what he sees when he sees me but I am pretty sure that it's got nothing to do with fucking or fighting, and sometimes he looks at me like this makes him angry, but other times, especially at the end of one of those shifts that are inexplicably twice as long as the rest, his eyes dart back and forth to my neither-male-not-quite-female chest, my short hair, my skinny legs, and I am pretty sure that the word for what happens to his semi-permanent forehead creases is relief. At moments like this, I almost love him. After all, he once worked out that we stand next to each other for more hours every week than he sleeps next to his wife. He blushed when he said this. He did not ask who I sleep with.

Shit, you're not paying me to talk about Garry. You're paying me to talk about what I saw with my own eyes. But here's the thing: I don't know.

I can tell you what I saw, the day before that, and the day before that, and the day before the day before the day you are paying me to talk about. What I saw was her trot towards Don't-Nuts. She was never, ever, looking at her phone, but straight ahead, at the fake plastic donuts that were forever in the window, though she wasn't straining towards them; she wasn't rushing or slacking; she just looked like she was where she was. So I never got why she then spent so long squinting at those plastic donuts. Once, I timed her: three minutes in front of the sugar rings, seven by the custards, eleven by the savouries. I kept expecting one of the teenagers who were stuck behind the actual donuts behind the counter inside the shop to come out and yell at her but they never did. In fact, one reason I agreed to take part in this documentary, aside from the money, was to find out what they thought about her, or if they could see her; those new double-custard donuts are pretty big and puffy, so it's likely they couldn't see outside their shop, at all. I also want to find out what donut she bought:

she'd eat it on her walk back to her office, but always with a long spoon, which she stuck into the paper bag, which the donut remained at the bottom of. It must've been one of the custards? Or the cheese fondue?

Anyway, that day, the day she just . . . *stopped*, it wasn't until a crowd began to gather that I saw that I was not seeing what I'd seen the day before, or the day before that, or the day before the day before that. As I walked towards the crowd, Garry grabbed my arm. 'It's a classic diversion tactic,' he said. 'Create a spectacle so you can go in and loot.' I turned back and looked where I was, after all, paid to look: into the shop. But it was just the same mix of bored teenage girls dabbing blusher onto the backs of their hands, exhausted mothers staring at nappies, and teenage boys looking at Lynx in the hope that no one would work out that what they really wanted to be looking at were condoms.

Then: heavy boots. I don't mean to sound melodramatic, but they sounded like Doom, you know, the one your conspiracy-theorist relatives are hoping for. But it was just MoreCity Security. They wear these platform boots with the MoreCity logo emblazoned on their steel toes. Kills me to say it, but they're pretty cool. Anyway, they parted the crowd the way I used to imagine Moses parted the Red Sea (actually no, I think I mean the way he did it in that Disney cartoon) and then, I saw her; how her feet were on the ground, but her body was leaning forward, as if she was about to fall, and yet – she didn't. Impossible, according to Newton, Einstein, those quantum mechanics dudes, the internet, my own eyes, Garry's eyes, etc. I saw them wave their walkie-talkies in her face. I saw one get down on his knees and plead. I saw the other push then pull her. I saw more and more people rush to see what everyone else wanted to see. 'It must be good,' someone shouted, 'if it's more fun than buying things or not-buying things.' I saw the police try and fail to remove her. Ditto, the fire brigade. When it was time for the Centre to close, I saw them succeed in removing the people who'd refused to stop looking at her.

I still can't tell you what I was looking at the moment she stopped. I mean, it looks, on the security footage, like I am looking at her; well, I'm not. I've been in this job a long time, too long, and I've mastered the art of looking like I am looking at what I'm meant to look at when I'm somewhere else. I could tell you that in the angle at which she scooped out her mystery donut filling with that long, thin spoon, I saw utopia: the one in which people didn't have to fill their holey souls with words like 'man,' 'woman,' 'queer' or 'straight.' Where people stopped pretending they were anything other than colanders. Yes, that would make metaphorical sense. In truth, however, there are too many thoughts between now and then for me to know. I could easily have been thinking about my friend Luca and why, even though my body plus their body equalled a sort of fizz that suggested we could get together, we never got together, and why this made me simultaneously sad and glad. Or about that wedding in that dream where the party favours consisted of psychedelic truffles called 'Top Gear.' (Luca said it must've been a queer wedding; straight people weren't that funny). Most likely it was my lunch I was thinking about, and whether today would be the day I traded in my soggy homemade sandwiches for a donut. Or something that had nothing to do with anything I've talked about so far, like shoelaces. Now, it is not just her stopping that seems impossible, but all of it: you, me, these thoughts, if thoughts is even the right word for what they are, and the fact that you are going to pay me for this. You are still going to pay me? Or do you want me to invent some detail – some small, gleaming detail which convinces everyone, if only for one blissful moment, that it will solve everything?

Barbara Glass, Colleague

Everything in this world happens for a reason, even toilet paper. It coming in perforated squares, I mean. *She*, however, did *not* get the memo; for weeks, there was always a half or a third of a square dangling from the dispenser once she'd finished her business.

It's not the sort of memo you want to spell out, of course you don't, it's vulgar, but as office manager, it was my duty —- and look up my job description if you don't believe me; the seventh bullet point is 'maintenance and optimisation of office sanitary facilities', which is a very long way of not saying toilet paper —- to not only spell but print it out and laminate it, too.

Even then, the behaviour continued. It put me off my cottage-cheese bap, I mean, right off.

Eventually, I was had to make the grave decision to turn around to her and say, 'did you not see the sign about the toilet paper.' She blinked at me. Then she looked back at her screen. As if I'd said nothing! The others, of course, had plenty to say about it; that I was over-fixated on other people's toilet habits, I'd gone too far, that S was clearly suffering some sort of mental health problems and there were for example private meeting rooms I could book if I wanted to discuss such sensitive topics, as I very well knew, the fifth bullet point of my job description being Room Booking Management. Have they since apologised to me? Have they said, Elaine, we're sorry, you were right about her all along, if only we'd listened to you? No, they have not. But that'll change once they discover that I've 'accidentally' ordered a year's supply of that really cheap, recycled toilet paper—you know, the stuff that just spreads your business around and about, and is certainly not perforated. I now have my own personal supply of triple-pleat, which I carry into and out of the toilet with me in a little red bag, and if the other girls are wondering whether I am on some sort of constant period, let them wonder. I am actually much happier this way.

Henry Altringham, Particle Physicist

Are you serious? You don't need a physics degree to solve the 'mystery.' You don't even need a GCSE. The answer is obvious: it's a hoax. The shopping centre was on the verge of closure, and now, lo and behold, it is so busy, you have to queue just to go inside. And I've no doubt you're in on it; I've seen your other 'documentaries'. It's just like the medieval monks: they always just *happened* to find some sacred remains when they really needed some cash. It's too convenient.

Mo Kinger, Assistant Assistant Manager, Don't-Nut

To be honest, I'd no idea she'd ever been to the shop. I don't look at the customers. What I look at are the donuts. I hated donuts before I started working here; now, I feel about them the way I feel about my sister's boyfriend's toenails, which are way too long. If I don't look at the donuts, I start to think about the customers, and how, once they've left the shop, I'll never see them again, or if I do, it will only be the same small part of them, the part that says, 'chocolate custard,' or, occasionally, 'hello,' or even, 'hellohowareyou-cheesefonduepleasethey'retoogood,' and what about the other parts, where do they go, where do I go when I am not the part that looks at the donuts then grabs the correct donut and places it into the correct bag, but not with my hands, with the self-disinfecting grabber, what if doing this same thing over and over eventually makes the other parts of me pack up and go to some holiday resort that is way too expensive for the rest of me to ever visit, not even after I get the Assistant Manager promotion, which Gregg, District Manager, says I will as soon as I get the hang of the self-disinfecting grabber, though I have to say that I am actually the master of the grabber.

What I mean is, I get carried away. If I think. About. Things. Too much.

It's happened since forever, but only once did anyone notice. Mrs Hazel, my Year Four teacher. She kept me behind, after school. I must've been, what, nine or ten. 'Something happens,' she said. 'You go . . . *off.*' Then she said something about me not feeling ashamed to be special. She told me to tell my mum but I didn't. The next parents' evening, I was scared she'd tell her, but she didn't, she just said I was quiet and got on with my work, and my mum smiled, and I felt like I'd got away with something, only I didn't know what it was, and if Mrs Hazel is out there watching, maybe she, you, could tell me – what was it that you saw? Where did I go?

Now, if you'll excuse me. You're standing in the way of the PlainAndSimples.

Hassan Al-Sabih, ToysRU Customer

I was on my way to buy my son a doll. The doll sang from its cheeks. It cost half my weekly salary. I'd only seen it on telly, and in my nightmares, and in the way my son's face moved when he talked about the way his life would be when he had the doll, which was sort of like the opposite of a nightmare, whatever the word for that is. Then – this person. They were sort of hovering over the tiles in the walkway between all the shops, as if they weren't actually a person but a recording of a person in a film and the person in control of the film had pressed pause. I looked up, half expecting to see a massive hand. I only saw pigeons, tons of them, flapping and crapping all over the head of that ugly horse (?) statue that's suspended from the ceiling on thin silver ropes. One of them crapped right in my eye. It stung. I yelled. No one helped me. I can't see! I can't see! Someone told me to stop yelling. Then someone else told me to move because thanks to me, they couldn't see anything, either. No, I said, I mean nothing. I see nothing. Just white. Just bird poop. Like snow, only, stickier. I can't tell you what happened after that because I still can't see anything. The doctors can't see any reason why I can't see anything. Another thing I can't do is get good at not-seeing things, like proper blind people, which makes my wife and everyone else think I'm faking it, but I mean, really, why would anyone fake such a thing? I hear the paused person is a woman is still stopped, and no one can move her, and even though she can't move to eat or blink or sleep or pee or poo or scratch her shameful places, she is still there, and no doctor or any other scientific person knows why, either. The reason I signed up for this programme is that I hoped someone might watch it who'd be able to solve such problems. Since then, my hope got a bit big for its boots, which are glittery and pink, by the way. Now, it's the person with their finger on the pause button I'm speaking to: can you press it for me, too? Please, just for a bit?

Wendy Li, Customer Services Assistant, ToysRU
For a long time, people came here not to shop, but to look at her. At Stophanie; at her body, just suspended, inches from the floor, always threatening to fall but never falling, never blinking, never sneezing, not when the dust on the floor piled up high enough to skim her nose, neither alive nor dead.

Sales dropped by 68, 89, then 247%, and even a blind man would've seen why; I did actually see not one not two but a whole fleet of blind men come here just to poke at her with their thin white sticks. Who could blame them?

Management said it was our fault. We did not do enough to *connect* with the customers. Now, we were to say, 'Good morning and how are you doing?' to every single person who walked into the shop. We were to say it with 100% sincerity, and if we didn't, we'd be fired. We chased out dozens of potential customers this way. One woman replied, 'Do you really want to know?' Then she told us that just that morning, her husband had asked for a divorce and she was kicking herself because for almost a decade she'd been dreaming of a divorce – or, more often, his sudden death – and he'd beaten her to it, and *beaten* was how she felt, she literally had bruises all over her abdomen as if she had been pummelled, not that he'd physically harmed her, he'd not even emotionally harmed her; it was just that she was bored of him, she was so very bored, but now that she'd finally got what she'd wanted, she did not feel interesting; she felt terrible and scared and alone and like something was rattling loose in her, and if we didn't believe her, the evidence was here, in this speech: before this morning, she'd have simply smiled and said, 'I'm very good, thank you.' None of the seven CSAs knew what to say to this. She smiled at us. Then she turned around and walked out. Another woman walked in, then another, then a man. The man asked about those singing dolls, the ones with the terrible cheeks, but we couldn't reply. It was as if that other woman's speech had done to us what had been done to Stophanie; by the end of the day, everyone was fired.

Rohan James, Don't-Nut Customer

I didn't know it but I was standing in the blind spot: the place where no security camera can see. So you'll have to believe me when I tell you that when I saw the, the, the, the, the   stop, I   cried.

Please forgive me. I suffer with   well they're not hic   cups

Not quite   aliisp   it's more like there are words I can't get out   words that want to getbetween the words I do   get out

Yes when I saw the   the   thethethe STOP, I,

I, I, I, I

Cried.

Honestly, I did. The look on her face; I'd never so much as dreamed of such peace.

Jenny Yates, Blogger and FlipFlop Gold Member Customer
Oh my god (suck, suck) thanks so much for contacting me was it because of my blog (suuucckk) did you see how many people see my blog can you imagine (suck) how many it's going to be once they've seen me on this okay okay no I know you're not (suck) paying me to talk about – what? Yeah, of course I'm not meant to say that you're paying me, that might make people suspect that I'm only saying what I'm saying because you're paying me and not, like the (suck suck) truth, but – surely you can edit it?
What? Chill out. Right. Yeah. So. Well, it was a normal day like any other. I was about to buy the new flavour of nail polish from FlipFlop. I'm on this nail polish diet only you see. The nail polish is kinda expensive but not compared to food, and you've got it with you all the time, so if you get hungry, you don't have to rummage in your back for a snack or whatever, you can just (suck, suck, suck).

Also there's a security guard in there, he's really hot, in kinda a girlish way, though also not, and if that makes me sound gay, I'm not, I'm not straight either, I'm all for equality love is love but I don't like want to put a (suck, suck) label on it, but anyway I have a bit of a thing for him and I am sure he has a thing for me and I kinda thought that living through a moment of historical adversity might make it happen you know (suck) outside of (suck, suck) my head, but the woman stopped and I stared at him, I

walked closer and closer and there was absolutely no way
he could've not seen me, yet somehow he continued to act
like he'd not seen me, 'Pretty surreal,' I said, and he said
nothing, so I said that I couldn't believe this was happening,
and then he looked up, I'd always imagined that when he
finally looked at me, I'd feel you know like (suck) *Seen* but
I just felt like I could've been any other person. 'Me either,'
he said, then he looked back at whatever he'd been looking
at before he'd been looking at me (something told me it
wasn't just Stophanie) and by then my brain was throwing me all these insane thoughts e.g. what if every human
in this world who thought they were so individual were
actually just different versions of the same boring person
e.g. what if every human was so different from every other
that they /we would never know each other at all and then
I realized I was super hungry I was so hungry I could eat
like every donut in that donut shop and so I went into that
donut shop I ordered a chocolate custard donut but what
did the idiot behind the counter give me? Coffee cream.
The absolute *worst*.

MoreCity Floor Manager
The problem with Stophanie is that she does not fall into
any of the 25 potential problems as outlined in the ACE
Floor Management course, which I attended at no incon-
siderable cost.

Gina Brown, Colleague
People will say that I don't know her but what they don't
know is that every day she bought a donut for lunch then
scooped out the filling with a long, thin spoon, which she

licked clean, then left in her desk drawer, along with the doughy part of her donut which I stayed longest in the office just to eat, I had previously bought my own donuts, and with fillings, too, but the girls told me off, and anyway, hers tasted better, I don't know why, I couldn't even tell you what fillings she went for, she was very meticulous in scraping them out, and although the longest conversation we ever had was at the Christmas party before the last Christmas party when she asked if I was excited and I said no, and then I knew that the time had come for me to ask something, but I couldn't, I find it very hard to talk to people, I definitely never thought I'd be talking to a camera about how I ate her uneaten donuts, or how sometimes, when she walked past my desk on the way to the toilet, her body oozed a sort of silence, and I'd have to stop typing, and – but I can't say what it was that happened, only that when it was over, my computer would be asleep, and she back at her desk, and then I'd shake my mouse, and in the last second of darkness, I'd be convinced, absolutely convinced, that she was leaving her donut-shells specifically for me, that our souls fit together the way enzymes and proteins fit together. Then, my screen would light. I'd click on my first new mail, then the second, then the third. Pretty soon, I'd forget I'd ever done anything else.

Same Difference

You're not sure if it's because you've been kissing for so long that you are starting to worry that your tongue might fall off or because the last time you kissed anyone for so long that you started to worry your tongue might fall off you were a teenager, and there are now more years between the age that you are now and the last of your teenage years than there are between your birth and their start; or because, right before you kissed, she said that you reminded her of someone, she didn't know who and yet, from the moment she saw you in the window seat—and not looking at your phone like a normal person but actually full on *staring* at the various other people in the bar, most of whom, it had to be admitted, this being a co-operatively run anarchist queer bar, were pretty interesting to look at—she had this feeling like time was cloning itself only the clone was actually travelling backwards in time, into the past, and you said, what, like the rowing boat at the end of *The Great Gatsby*, and she said it was years since she'd read it and she hadn't even remembered that bit, but now that you mentioned it, she could literally *feel* something moving around in her chest, just like she when she'd first read it, which is what, actually, she was talking about, the way she felt when she first looked at you, which was maybe an intense thing to say on a first date but fuck it, she *was* queer after all, she could be the fuck however she wanted; or because the second to last person you dated said that you reminded them of their cousin's best friend they'd had a crush on as a kid, only, they said it right after you fucked and you said, what, so I am just a way for you to fulfil your fantasy and they said all love was a fantasy and you said, but it makes me feel used, and then they said a lot about what some queer theorist said about love being the only experience for which people were prepared to change themselves in order to sync up with another human, and they talked for so long that by the time they'd finished, you assumed they must be right, even if the word 'sync' then made you think about the times when your phone refused to pair with your bluetooth speaker even when it was literally nudging the speaker in the way the cat sometimes nudged your book out of your hand to get your attention; or because so many of the people in this bar are wearing the exact same dungarees as you, whilst others are wearing the jeans and baggy-but-edgy t-shirt you wear on most non-date days, whilst even those that are wearing the sorts of preppy shirts you'd never wear have the same short hair and glasses as you—but you feel less like an individual than how you imagined, after spending half a day down a wiki-hole on the topic, a worker ant might feel—a joyful acceptance of the incompleteness of the both/and relation of their body to the whole—only, you weren't working, except maybe to locate the glitch that would break down the pseudo-hive that was gender, which was probably what a lot of these other queers were now thinking about, only, they probably weren't thinking of it as a pseudo-hive, which may or may not mean that the neural or affective or whatever the fuck they were pathways that led you to this particular metaphor is what is particular about you.

'I can't believe you're kissing with your eyes open.' There is a lot of spit round her mouth; she wipes it onto her sleeve.

'I wasn't.'

'You were! I saw it.'

'Then you must've had your eyes open, too.'

She opens her mouth to speak, then shuts it, starts to laugh. 'I guess we're both freaks.'

Then someone spits the word 'rhizome' onto the back of your neck. It smells like the vegan chicken they serve here, and even though, when you ordered said chicken last week, you complained that it tasted like the vegan chicken from Morrison's budget range and speculated that the two-hour wait was not because the skinny vegan chef was 'hand-crafting' each piece of chicken according to a 'bespoke recipe' but actually running to and from Morrison's, you can somehow tell that the vegan chicken this person has just eaten or is possibly still eating is from here.

And then you open your mouth to tell her all this, only for your tongue, which feels much sturdier than it did at the start of whatever it is this is, to venture into her mouth—as if it's there that it truly belongs.

People Also Ask

Are You a Boy or a Girl?
I have a vagina. I don't shave it—not because of feminism, or whatever, but because I can't be bothered. (Which is the sort of thing a boy would say if a boy had a vagina).

Why Did You Lose the Orienteering Competition?
My feet are too big for Google Maps. (They (may (or may not)) belong to a boy who is sitting on the sofa of a girl he's on a Tinder date with, only this girl looks like a boy and her cat looks like a demon, its claws are cutting straight through his jeans, and she's saying: Are You Not A Cat Person, Then? She laughs like this has some secret meaning. The boy wants to cry. The boy wants to cry even though he's not the sort of boy who cries or who likes girls who look like boys or like cats with secret meanings   he does not like secrets   he does not like meanings   he does not like how his head is filling with all these words he does not like). The rest of me is just a girl whose eyelashes won't stick to mascara.

U OK, Hun?

Why Are There No Plants In Your House, Not Even A Cactus?

There *was* a plant (generic, green) but I was too busy looking for you to look after it. Then I found you, your compass was pointing at the space between my legs, there was a map on the inside of my left arm but I was too busy looking at the space between your boobs to read it (I was always too busy) and you left.

You said you were coming back but none of the bodies in my body believed it.

My feet were too cold to be the boy's feet but my fingers were hungry in the way only boys are allowed to be hungry, they were crying in the way not even girls are allowed to cry, and I WhatsApped you but you didn't reply, and I looked for food but there wasn't any, and it was Sunday, so there was no hope of buying any, and then you Voicenoted me to say you'd just crammed a slice of your niece's birthday cake into your mouth and it smelt like my secret meaning and now all the other totally straight and normal people at the party were eating it and saying oh isn't it delicious? So fresh, so moist! And you were *dying*.

You were dying but my plant was already dead—it had probably been dead since way before I met you but I'd only just noticed. So I fried its leaves with some avo and jackfruit that I found not in the fridge but behind it. The boy said I was a dickhead, the girl (what girl?) said she was only here for the cake which tasted of secret meaning. I said this was all they were getting. They gave me their most withering stares (which weren't that withering). They ate it anyway.

Is This Your Idea Of An Explanation?
My only regret is the avo: it's best served cold.

You Should Probably Try A Cactus.
Fine.

So What Style of Attachment Would You Call This?

I WAS ONLY four minutes late, but Fran was already sat down, a beer in one hand, a sausage roll in the other.

I thought you weren't going to come, she said.

Four minutes late is basically on time. I slid onto the bench opposite her.

I know, she said, but I'm *basically* a pessimist, though a hopeful one.

I get it, I said, like if you expect the worst, nothing can disappoint you, ever?

She opened her eyes cartoonishly wide and said, how did you know? Then she chomped down on her sausage roll. She really did chomp, mouth open, pink post-sausage mash in full view. Although I'd only just eaten, I suddenly felt faint, as if my stomach had been empty for days.

You want one, she announced.

How did you know?

She grinned. Let's just say I have an instinct for other people's suppressed instincts.

Over two more rolls, four pints and three packets of crisps, we talked about being queer but neither vegan nor a fan of *Ru Paul's Drag Race*, both of which the cishets seemed to think queerness consisted of; what it consisted of, neither of us could be sure, but huge backpacks, too much therapy, and the desire for the impossible, were certainly in there. We talked, only, it did not feel like talking, it felt as if we were already inside each other's bodies, as if we had been living inside of them our whole lives, we were merely reminding ourselves of it.

When a silence finally bloomed between us, I leaned into it.

She scooted away.

Sorry, she said. It's not—she sighed with a degree of concentration that made me certain this was a Strategy she'd worked out with her therapist.

There's something you should know. Something about me. Sadness dribbled down her cheeks and I wanted to lick it off. I wanted to chomp it down. I wanted to poop it out.

Oh?

She stood up. Come to the toilets.

Maybe she had a kink. Yes, I thought, as we bundled into a cubicle, she was surely about to pull a rope or a butt plug out of her backpack.

I usually wait until at least the third date to share this, she said, but, and I'm sorry if this is too much, but it feels as if you, us, this date, is made, you know, of a *different substance*.

I tried, again, to kiss her, but she held up her hand in the manner of a traffic warden.

Slowly, and without meeting my eye, she unbuttoned her shirt. Something poked out from between the buttons—a hook. It jutted out from the space between her boobs, like an almost third boob, except that it was nothing like a boob; it was fleshy, yes, but thin and pointy, and it dangled right down to her thighs.

I'd never seen anything like it, I'd never dreamed of anything like it, and yet, just looking at it made my body feel like my body in a way I had long since stopped hoping was possible. I wanted to cry.

At this point, she said, people usually run. The few who don't, well, she smiled at a square of toilet paper glued to the floor, they get too attached.

I reached towards her but she backed towards the sanitary bin.

I mean it. We'll *literally* be joined together. She stared at the 'Date not working out? Ask for Angela' sticker. It's not easy.

I didn't care about easy. I'd never felt anything for anyone that wasn't overshadowed by doubt. Yeah they're hot, my brain would usually whisper, *but they're a bit pedantic, and their washing-up style is very different to yours, and sometimes when they ask if you want a cup of tea, you want to smack them*. But I wanted Fran in the unambiguous and bodily way I'd wanted that sausage roll. I pulled her towards me. As our lips smashed together, I felt a short, sharp scratch, almost as if I was having a blood test, even though I wasn't, and the scratch wasn't in my arm, it was in my chest, and when I tried to pull away, we smashed foreheads.

Told you, she said. Then she unbuttoned my shirt and I unbuttoned hers and she pushed me back against the metro tiles, which were cold and slippery and hard, and we fucked.

Her flat would, in my previous life, have been a five-minute walk away, but in our new (but old-feeling) state, it took us almost twenty. If one of us walked too fast, or strayed more than a foot from the other, a pain would rip through the other's chest, and she'd yell, and people would stare, and we'd stare back, and the people would transfer their stare to the floor in the hope that this would make us doubt whether they'd even noticed us, and we'd move on. I was quite a bit taller than her, so it took us a while to synchronise our pace.

We walked through her front door, and through all interior doors, at a right angle.

I'm desperate for a shit, she said, and I could already sense she was about to speed up, so I sped up, too, and we scuttled into her bathroom, like some mutant crab. There was, I noticed, an unusually large space between the sink and the toilet.

Squat there, she commanded, with your back turned.

I obeyed. I tried not to listen to the plop.

I hadn't needed a shit before, but now I did—almost as if her needs were travelling through the hook. I didn't even have to tell her this: she flushed, took one look at my face, and assumed what, only a few moments before, had been my position.

Before Fran, I'd never dated anyone for more than eight months, I'd never lived with a partner, I'd only said *I love you* twice. 98% of my dates ended firmly in the Friend Zone. So when my friends, many of them having come into my life as potential dates, found out we'd already moved in together, they were shocked. Shocked and appalled! *It's just not like you*, said one. *I'm worried.*

What they couldn't seem to understand was that before Fran, I'd felt as if I had an almost-empty fruit bowl where my self ought to be. The 'almost' consisted of a rotting banana and three crispy clementine leaves. The bowl was made out of fake wood, on offer from Wilko. I woke up most days disappointed that my body, despite this lack, was still here, still in need of all the things bodies need. I woke up late, usually too late to shower before my first meeting, I ate lunch at 11am or 3pm or never, and by 'lunch' I mean a few spoonfuls of Tupperware leftovers, eaten cold, and whilst standing in front of the fridge. I frequently went days without leaving the house. People thought I was vibrant, but that's because talking was my No.1 strategy— developed without the input of any therapist—to distract from the fruit-bowl feeling.

Now, I sprang out of bed and into running shoes, I ran around the park, or, if I was feeling particularly energetic, to the woods, or, if it was a weekend, to the cafe on the other side of the woods, which sold delicious coffees and pastries. Fran had been doing these things for years, and whilst I hadn't touched a running shoe since school, I took to it like *a dog to water*, she said. Or, I said, like a duck to air, because ducks like air, they sleep on the shore, with their beaks tucked into their wings, and she laughed, and then we stopped by the pond to ventriloquise their dreams. I ate lunch when she ate lunch, which was at 1pm, out of sight from our laptops, hearty, and warm. We both worked from home; living together was easy, so long as we scheduled our calls at different times. If I felt bored or tired or lonely or scared, I'd only have to brush the hook with my pinky finger, and the feeling would go, and then a space would open up; I didn't know what, if anything was in it, only that it would fill with the future any minute now. Any minute now!

The weirdest thing was that no one noticed the hook—not strangers in the park, not the man in the corner shop, not our friends.

Fran didn't think it was weird. They'll think we're just like any other coupley couple. The hook is so thin, so stretchy, that no one can see it; their brains filter out anything they don't expect to be there.

As a test, we both wore tank tops to a brightly-lit bar, angling our bodies so that the hook looked almost like a glow stick, or a rod of lightning, which I decided to interpret as a sign that we were soon to reach the future the hook had been promising.

We talked to our friends, who were sitting opposite us. We glanced at the hook between sentences. We even asked them, a few drinks in, whether there was anything they noticed.

No, said the friends, looking worried. Why? Are you pregnant?

We laughed and laughed and laughed.

Now they looked annoyed. Seriously, what is it?

Oh, we said, it's nothing. Absolutely nothing.

Later that night, the friends sent me a message to say, *we like Fran, but we are starting to wonder if we'll ever see you alone again. We miss you.*

They were stupid, so stupid. What, or who, was there to miss? The thought of my body, unattached to any other, was too sad to bear. Plus, Fran's fruit bowl was made from olive wood that was unquestionably real, and replete with fruit that was unquestionably perfect.

The perfection, of course, didn't last. I thought it would, and when it didn't, I thought that telling this story from the perfect angle might revive it, at least for the time of the telling. But these words are sugar-sticky; there isn't a sentence I can mash into them that shows which part of what happened next happened first, or how, or why.

There was the night when I sat up—the 'I need to pee' signal—when she pulled me back down to the mattress. Hold it in, she mumbled, I'm having an exceptional dream. When I tried to move, she gripped my wrist so tight I could still see the outline of her fingers in the morning.

There was the day I suggested we go to a craft fair and she said that she hated craft fairs and so did I, I just spent all my time criticising the art, which wasn't really art, more like imitation, and done badly, and I said, what if I enjoy the criticism, and she said, well I don't, I want to go the garden centre, and so we went to the garden centre, and I pretended to myself that I wasn't pretending to her that I didn't hate garden centres.

There was the night when she asked if I wanted a cup of tea, a cup of the loose-leaf oolong she usually saved for special occasions, at least, she used to, but every moment with me felt so special it blew the concept of the 'occasion' out of the water—she asked me all this, and I wanted, what I really wanted, was to smack her.

There was the day I fancied a biscuit only half an hour after breakfast, I jumped out of my seat, but she didn't follow.

Ouch. She clutched her chest. Holy fuck.

Sorry.

She scowled at me, I mean really scowled, like a character in a 1950s children's book. You can't accept that we're two different people, with different wants, different needs.

Sorry, I said. I'm really sorry.

I sat back down. I didn't move until she stood up for a pee. I didn't need to pee, I peed anyway, it smelt like anger, not mine but hers. In the split second between my flushing and her standing up, I saw myself as I used to be, peeing, alone, or perhaps in the semi-company of my phone. I felt sick. I felt as if I didn't have a body to be feeling sick or anything with. It took me a few days, which felt like years, to identify this feeling as homesickness, a further week for me to attach to the feeling the words: I want. I want, *I want to get away from her.*

But I couldn't transform words into non-words, I couldn't remember what non-words were. When she asked if I wanted to celebrate our three-month anniversary by returning to the bar where we'd first met, I didn't say yes, I didn't say no, and when she asked if I had an alternative suggestion, I said I don't know, and when she said that it wasn't fair to make her do all the emotional labour of making decisions, I said sorry, and when she told me to stop saying sorry and start changing my behaviour, I said that whenever I wanted anything that she didn't want, she shot me down, and she stopped walking so abruptly that my chest skin ripped.

Ouch.

Sorry, I'm sorry, it's just, I would never *shoot you down*, I'd never shoot anyone down, I've been a pacifist since I was seven and a half. Then she pushed me into the bar. You have to order.

There were twelve beers on tap, two ciders, and five flavours of sausage roll, four of them vegan.

When the cishets queuing behind us began to grunt and cough, she elbowed me. It's not life and death. Just choose.

I said pale ale, I said chorizo, I said chorizo and red pepper, I did not say that my words weren't real because my 'I' wasn't, I was a fruit bowl again, only, it no longer contained a rotten banana, it no longer contained three crispy clementine leaves, it was completely, I mean *completely*, empty.

Good choice, she said, when we'd eaten our sausage rolls.

But when she leant towards me, I climbed up onto the bench so quickly that she screamed, she screamed so loud that all the cishets stopped talking, but I didn't care, I wanted someone, anyone, to witness how weird this had been, because it had *been*, it was over, the future we'd been promised was in the past, how it had got there without ever touching our present, I didn't know, I still don't, I'm sorry. I said I was sorry. I can't do this anymore.

Oh no, she said, you're just scared, people always are, at this point, the point where we are really getting to know each other, the *real* other, not the mirage.

She was crying and I was crying, and every time I

moved, she screamed, and every time she screamed, I moved, and then I jumped onto the floor, and the cishets parted like the sea for Moses, and I did feel a bit like Moses, like I was headed towards the end of an important story, I didn't look back I just pushed open the outside doors and when they slammed behind me I felt—

—but there isn't a word.

There isn't a word that can describe what happened, there isn't a word that can describe how what happened was tangled up with what didn't happen, how I ran and we stretched and I chomped and we ripped and we tore and we bled. We bled all over the floor, which was, at least, tiled.

Fucking hell.

I'd accidentally run into the smoking area. A cishet bloke was staring at my chest. We were wearing the same plaid shirt with red and black squares.

Did you get stabbed?

Blood was blurring my reds and my blacks into the same purplish brown.

I'm not sure.

The doctors didn't believe me when I said there was no weapon, no aggressor. There were just two bodies moving towards, and then away from, each other. There was the time their wants had skipped in the same direction; there was that time's ending; there was my inability to notice the ending until we were already in the middle of something else.

They gave me dressings and infusions and stitches and pills. Nothing worked: the hole, which was just bigger than needle-sized, and right between my breasts, continued to bleed. They sent me home with a month's supply of dress-ings; it would heal by then, and if it didn't, I'd learn to live with it, people did.

That was two years ago, and whilst the bleeding's stopped, the healing hasn't, every day the scar is a little bigger than the day before, and by bigger I mean longer; I mean, it's too long to fold into my sports bra, or into a dating App message. I mean I'd love to do what Fran did. I'd love to just unbutton my shirt and say, there's something you should know. But if I've learned anything from this, it's that I'm not Fran. I'm not Fran, and when my next girlfriend leans in to kiss me, I'll let her. I'll press my chest against her chest, closer and closer, until I feel it, the moment I miss most of all: that first scratch—so sharp, so short.

More Than Not-Sweeping

Behind us there were sand dunes, and on the sand dunes were tufts of brown grass, which made me think of those almost-bald men who thought that if they schuzzed up their few remaining hairs with wax or gel, no one would think of them as the men who were almost bald. I didn't know how schuzzed was spelled - the 's' was pronounced more like a 'j'—or whether spelling rules existed for words that existed only in hair salons many miles from any dictionary. I asked K what she thought, but she looked at me as if her life was ruined and I was the cause, and although I knew that such looks were her brain's attempt to relieve her from the truth, i.e. the ruin was larger and more complex than we'd ever know, and that thinking that I knew what everyone thought was another such attempt, I began to feel like I'd swallowed something that ought never to be swallowed—like sand. I coughed and coughed.

'Why are you Not Sweeping?' Senior Leadership yelled through the rolled-down window of her Jeep, the wheels of which were doing to the sand what those imaginary bald men had been doing to their hair. My throat ached—evidence that the sand was as real as it was meta-phorical: small comfort.

My broom, it's true, was on the ground, but I'd no idea how it had got there.

'I've swept 25 litres in the last twelve minutes!' K waved her broom triumphantly; it looked unbearably wet and sorry for itself.

'That's—' Senior Leadership was nearer to the ground than us, and yet, when she looked at us, she looked down-wards. Whether this was a cause or a consequence of her position, I would never know. '—satisfactory.' She licked her lips and swallowed, as if in physical discomfort. 'But satisfactory is not good enough; nor is *good* good enough; you might be expecting me to say that outstanding is good enough, but that is exactly the sort of attitude that results in people forgetting that if they stop sweeping whilst they are being paid what I should remind you is *above* average wage for sweeping, they will soon, if they do not get a hold of their attitude, not be a sweeper, and therefore no longer a person, at all.' to do with value - lucy

Her cart's wheels szujjed the sand again; I coughed, again; again, everything felt like sand. No. *I* felt like sand. I felt like an egg timer where the internal sand is clumping together, refusing to do what some human has decided it has been put on this earth to do.

'Hurry.' K shoved my broom at my chest. 'I can see right through your foot.'

I looked, and whilst there would have been a time when I could've told myself that the translucency of my toes was a Senior Management construct designed to discourage idleness, that my personhood was in no way contingent on my ability to sweep or not, such an idea was now as difficult to access as the almost-bald man's hair, and as I reached for the broom, I was sure, absolutely sure, that it really was what I'd been put on this earth to do.

Forty-two minutes later, sand splattered the back of my neck. 'Seventy-five litres already.' Senior Management flung a Gold Star out of her window. 'Good,' she said, 'but not quite good enough.' Then, she left.

'I did 30 litres in 27 minutes yesterday,' said K, 'and she didn't even give me a Special Mention.' Her lip was wobbling, as if she might cry, and that thing happened when she looked not like my Chosen One, my companion, my love, etc, etc, but like any random person; I juggled the star in an attempt to forget this.

'It's all made up,' I said. The star was silky soft against my cheek, yet I squeezed it and squeezed it, determined to find out what filled its soft, round belly. 'None of it means anything.'

'Then why are you smiling so much?'

'I'm not.' Pressing the star to my skin made my 'I' feel real in the way my toes now did.

'Sometimes, I think —' She was now crying whilst sweeping, which was an extreme form of feeling whilst sweeping, which was even worse than thinking whilst sweeping, which was the number one cause of people no longer being sweepers and therefore persons —'that no matter how hard I try, I'll never be Good, not even for a minute, there's some trick to it I'm missing and only no one will tell me what it is, not even you, even though we are meant to tell each other everything.'

I wanted to tell her that there was no secret, or if there

was, I didn't know it; but I was squeezing the star, which was suddenly the most important thing, more important than sweeping, or Senior Management, or men who refused to see that other people might see them as bald. I dropped the broom and, with both hands, I squeezed and squeezed; the tide lapped at my ankles, then, at my knees; finally, my palms began to hurt, and I opened my eyes, and I saw a flaccid rubber thing in my palm that did not look like it had ever been anywhere near any star. Then I looked up, past K, at the other sweepers; they swept the water back into itself only for it to lap back towards them, and they did not look like people, but like those thin metal hair grips that almost-bald men wore in their dreams.

'No more rewards for you.' Senior Management was back. 'They go straight to your head.'

'What about—'

Senior Management stepped on the accelerator as K said 'me'.

Then came an announcement that anyone who swept more than 56.5l of water in the next 25 minutes would win an extra Happy Hour. K picked up her own broom, and mine. She swept 59.2 l of water in 25 minutes, but because she used my brush as well as her own, this was recorded as only 29l each, and so the extra Happy Hour was awarded to T, who did not attempt to hide his smugness as he scarpered over the dunes.

'Oh well, we've only forty-five minutes left,' said K, now brushing the sea in the manner of a human who was far better acquainted with the word 'tired' than was sensible. 'What shall we do after our shift?'

I looked at the place where the water met the sky; I

suppose it's what, in the time before The Ruin, might've been called the horizon. For a moment, I saw that world, the one in which there was more to life than sweeping and not sweeping, by which I mean less, by which I mean, in this other world, such words did not exist; whether this world had anything to do with bald heads, I cannot say. I thought I was going to tell K all about it, but when I tried, I said, 'Let's watch TV.' I said, 'takeout,' I said, 'fuck then takeout whilst watching TV.' I said, 'why is it that the closer you get to the end of something, the slower time moves?'

'Sweep,' she said, 'it'll go faster.'

And I did. I swept with one hand whilst clutching the deflated star in the other; soon, we were on the dry side of the dunes, rubbing our bodies against each other, as if they and we would never sweep, ever again.

Sex, Drugs and Dead Birds

THE BIRDS KEPT dying. They kept dropping out of the sky and splatting onto the pavement. They were a Sign—of what, I didn't know. I documented them on my phone in the hope they would make their meaning clear, if not to me, then to one of my friends.

It was to this end that I showed Julie the video of the dead magpie and its mate screaming from the branch of a nearby tree. The scream was the kind of terrible that cannot be squashed into words. I was premenstrual. A few seconds of it, and my face was mostly tears.

Tears? Julie pressed my phone to her ear. Traffic, she said, was the only noise *she* heard, and even though she knew, intellectually, that it was part of the slow violence that was late capitalism that would eventually destroy this planet and all the ideas in it, she could not quite feel it. She may have said more words. Or she may not. All I know is that at the word 'planet', she made the face which meant she either wanted to slap me or fuck me, and my body emptied of everything besides the question: which?

Then Carolyn arrived, expelling one of those long, tremulous sighs we believed was a reminder that she was a mother and thus higher up the scale of legitimate suffering than us. Have you made any progress on the next Change?

Alas, said Julie, catching my eye, we have not.

Carolyn shook her head. You know, I joined this group as a way of developing my identity *outside* of motherhood but—and don't take this the wrong way—you all act like children.

Ed, Ben and Mags sidled up to us, wielding a huge banner between them.

Ta-da!

I had to admit that with their colourful backpacks, rosy cheeks and self-satisfied smiles, *children* was the first word they brought to mind.

But did we not agree, said Carolyn, that we're a Post-Banner Action Group?

Err . . . Mags flicked through her notebook. There's no record of it in the Minutes.

Mags only minuted suggestions she personally agreed with; everyone knew this, yet no one could be bothered to do it themselves, not even Carolyn.

Julie made a face at the banner, one I was sure she would not be capable of making were she not doing a PhD in— something. It filled my brain with images of the ways we could fuck each other.

This banner, she said, communicates the joy of the radical child. It is the sort of visual information that effectively transports the observer in the direction of fun.

Carolyn looked up from her phone and said, this might be news to you, but life isn't all about fun.

But fun, said Ed, is what capitalism promises—

—And the patriarchy, chipped in Ben, looking pleased with himself.

—Yes, said Ed, looking less pleased, *and* the patriarchy. The point is, the only way we can convince people is if we promise more fun than they're already having.

Carolyn shook her head. This isn't the point of our Movement.

I thought we weren't calling ourselves a Movement?

A long argument ensued.

I'm not sure I'd have sat through it had Julie not looked at me with that fuck-you-or-slap-you look three more times.

Mags minuted 'Promise more fun' and 'Also the patriarchy.'

When Carolyn ended things by signalling that it was time she pestered her daughter to feed the guinea pigs her partner had bought her for Christmas, never considering that she, of course, would be the one to do the work of keeping the stupid thing alive, Julie poked my arm. Want a drink . . . Somewhere else? She was looking at me like she wanted to fuck me, definitely fuck, not slap. But the me who'd imagined all the ways I could fuck her was gone. I walked around the corner from the bar and, when I was absolutely sure no one could see me, I called an Uber.

◊

I did not see any dead birds for ages after that, not even on the day I lost my job, which was also the day of our next meeting. You would think something serious like losing your job would shake your mind free of frivolous thoughts, e.g. birds falling out of the sky and what that might mean.

But no. My eyes scurried all over the pavement as I walked; the pavement, but also the gutter, the kerb, garden walls, those random patches of grass outside office blocks. When I found only empty cans and 'fuck the EU' graffiti and empty crisp packets and 'fuck you for fucking us over' graffiti and empty baggies and illegible graffiti, I tried not to feel disappointed.

Julie didn't understand why I was more bothered by the absence of dead birds than the presence of anti-EU graffiti.

It was then that I told her about the job.

What? They can't get rid of you for no reason.

They can and they did.

You could take them to court.

But I've got to pay the rent, and even if I didn't, it's a hassle.

She looked me a look I did not care to analyse.

So ironic, she said, a *charity* treating its employees like shit. But you could at least write a letter to the *Guardian*.

I checked her face for signs that she was joking; she was not.

Carolyn extended her neck in my general direction and said, Julie's right. I've at least three friends who have direct debits with that charity; they've a right to the truth.

By this point, not only Julie and Carolyn, but Ed, Mags and Ben were throwing sincerely sympathetic stares in my direction. For years I had dreamed of this moment: the one when my suffering was externally legitimised. I had imagined it would make me feel real. Well, it didn't. It filled me with a despair so compelling I went at least three hours without looking at my phone.

◊

On the second day of my temp job, I saw a dead rat. I did not photograph it. I texted Julie to tell her. But, I added, the good news is, I've checked with Derrida, and it's NOT a Sign. Five and a half hours later—hours which, since no one had given me any work, I mostly worried that Derrida wasn't the one who wrote about Signs, but some other French-theory bro, maybe Lacan or Barthes—she replied with a laughing emoji. It wasn't sincere though; the part that knew this was the same part that knew the dead rat was not a Sign in the way that the dead-but-not-dead magpie most definitely *was*.

◊

Finally, it was the day of Change. It was a Saturday. We circled our city's pedestrianised shopping street. We had no banners. We did not stamp or shout. As we walked, we muttered 'other ways.' We had spent at least one whole meeting debating whether or not to have microphones, deciding, in the end, not, because microphones would make us look deliberately performative, causing the shoppers to place us in the category of buskers or protesters, whereas our aim was to stretch the category in which they placed themselves until, breaking, it revealed the nothingness at its core. What we had not considered were the real buskers, how many there were, or how loudly their amps projected worn-out renditions of 'Hey Jude'. Nor had we considered how dizzying it was to actually walk in circles vis. talk about walking in circles whilst sitting still.

A few people walked into us or shouted at us for walking into them before hurrying into the nearest shop. Julie spotted some teenage boys filming us from the doorway of JD Sports. They probably thought we'd escaped from an institution.

That's a stereotypical and quite frankly offensive thing to say, said Carolyn. She did not look offended; her mouth was threatening to smile with relief at having something to correct. Her daughter, Skye, shot Julie a knowing look, which she missed.

Are we nearly there yet? asked Ben.

Mum banned us from saying that, said Skye.

Ben said he was joking.

Ed said he was going to throw up.

Carolyn said we'd stop when we knew we'd made a Change.

Ed said, again, that he was going to throw up.

Julie asked how we would know when the Change had been made, and whether or not it was Capitalised.

I wanted to suggest we ask the Jehovah Witnesses, who were shooting us pitiful glances from the doorway of Debenhams, but Carolyn said that being facetious was not going to help anyone.

Julie said she wasn't being facetious. Her eyes lingered on the mannequin in the Top Shop window, whose thin legs and baggy trousers I had already wasted a lot of effort trying not to want. It was time, she said, making her Deep PhD face, to accept we had, on this occasion, failed.

Ed threw up.

Carolyn sighed. You've really ruined things now. She

tugged her daughter away from the sick. I better get going. Skye's got an Expressive Dance competition.

When they were a few steps away from us, Skye said, Mummy, that wasn't fair, he couldn't help it if his food wanted to come out of his belly!

The silence that followed Carolyn's departure was thrilling, vomit or no vomit.

Ben suggested we go for a drink.

Julie's eyes said: fuck me fuck me. And her mouth: let's shop.

You two shop then, said Ed, we'll see you in the pub.

You're really going to drink? I asked.

The Change, said Ed, is *within*. His cheeks were green.

Then, it was just me, Julie and Topshop's pumping techno. She marched up to a rail of sequinned bodies as if they had been her destination all along. Then she narrowed her eyes at my body. Unzip your coat.

I unzipped my coat.

This would look good on you. She pressed the body against my chest.

Are you. Actually. Kidding.

We stared at each other for as long as we ever had, and I thought: maybe she's right. Maybe I can live in a body which wears sequinned bodies.

Then she burst out laughing. Course I am.

Good.

By the time we made it to the changing rooms, I had nine clothing items to try and little memory of my past life. I saved the mannequin's trousers to last, as did Julie. We stood, side by side, in the changing room mirror, frowning.

Maybe they'd look better if we swapped sizes?

OK.

She pulled off her trousers, revealing two perfectly shaved legs and a pair of lacy pants, whose borders were pube-free.

Come on then.

I pulled off my trousers to reveal two legs that were dotted with stubble and in-growing hairs and patches of raw, red skin I could never be bothered to moisturise, just as I could never be bothered to trim my pubes, or replace the M&S pants my mum had bought me three years ago, whose elasticated leg holes, the mirror informed me, were fraying.

These look wrong, too, she said.

It saddened me to admit she was right. But I didn't move from the mirror. Neither did she. I looked at her looking at me looking at her looking at me looking at her and hoping—even though I knew this was as pointless as buying new clothes or walking in circles to stop other people buying new clothes—that I would one day find out what her looks meant and that, when I did, they would mean what I wanted them to mean, and so would begin a new era of peace.

Then she pulled out her phone and a shiver ran down my spine as the window of opportunity in which we might have fucked slammed shut.

They're at Ponk, she said, her eyes on the screen.

Ponk was the co-operatively run anarchist bar where we held our meetings.

Of course they are.

Apparently there's a band on . . . and they're . . . *good*?

I returned to my own cubicle and my own clothes, and when I handed all nine items to the shop assistant, I felt mostly relieved.

The band was not good, not even after a beer. After a second beer, they were worse. After a third, they were irrelevant.

After a hefty dab of MD, they were talented interpreters of joyful melancholia, as observed by Ed, who I found myself liking way more than usual. I found myself finding no problem whatsoever with notions such as finding yourself.

Then Julie's hand found my hand and it pulled the rest of me away from Ed. Let me guess, was he exposing the uniquely troubled nature of his soul? Was he confirming your own uniqueness?

The only words in my head were, 'My hand is sweaty,' and so I said them and she laughed and I said sorry. She squeezed my hand harder and turned towards me. I thought: this is the moment we kiss. Then she said that she loved how MD filled her with a love which satisfied itself, not like when you fancied someone and the more you did it, the more you wanted of them, more and more . . .

Sometimes, I said, meaning *always*, I worry that you are omniscient.

No. She stared at a stranger's empty beer glass. I just perform my knowledge to distract people from the fact that I'm less real than them.

But I've always worried *I'm* the least real.

You? What? You're *so* real.

We laughed; I stopped first. You do realise, I said, we're doing exactly what you said Ed was doing to me?

She squinted, as if searching for the memory attached to a Facebook memory from several years ago. *Shit*. She let go of my hand and wiped her hand on her jeans and sat up and opened her eyes so wide I thought they would pop but they didn't. You know, she said, I had therapy for a while. And it was the same as studying. You get good at spotting patterns, you mostly understand them, but you can't dream up alternatives, or if you try, they turn to nothing. Like this morning. Ha.

My phone beeped. My head suddenly tingled with memories of the many people I loved but hadn't seen for ages. Surely one of them had got in touch. But no. My phone was simply whining that its memory was full. Now Julie was speaking to somewhere else. Mags sat down beside me and said it had happened, the Change, she could feel it, we had done Something, we should be proud. I did not say that all we'd done was get high; I smiled and I nodded and I deleted seventy-two photos. Eventually she left and Julie returned and I told her I'd deleted all my photos bar the birds.

Your birds, she said, grabbing my hand again, what are they *really* about?

The birds are just birds.

But nothing is *just* anything. You know that. I know that you know that.

We had somehow travelled backwards in time to all the moments we could have kissed but didn't but this time we did.

When the others picked up more drugs, we fucked

through our comedown. We fucked in her bed, which smelt of damp paper. I did not worry about the hairiness of my legs vs the smoothness of hers; I worried that wrenching our fuck from fantasy to reality had made it—even as she made me come and I made her come and she kissed my neck and I licked the groove between her breasts—less real, not more. I worried what all this worrying said about me.

I needed that, was the first thing she said, when it was over.

I tried to say, *me too*. But my jaw was otherwise engaged, so I curled my arm around her waist and spooned her from behind and pressed my lips against her back. For a second, maybe two, I was certain she knew what I meant. Then she wriggled to the far side of the bed. Please leave. Her tone announced that the time for questions was over. So I did it. I left.

On my way home, I saw three dead birds—two pigeons and one brown bird whose species, even after an extensive Google search, I failed to identify. No one screamed for any of them, not even me. I messaged Julie a photograph with the caption: Coincidence . . . or Sign? LOL. She 'saw' my message twenty-three minutes after I'd sent it. She did not reply.

She continued to not-reply all through the next week, even though I stared at our message thread on my phone almost constantly, even though #deadbirds was now trending on Twitter. They'd been dying in the paths of other people, too. Some of these people were scientists and a few of these scientists admitted that they didn't know why it was happening—and it was happening more and more—but that it was probably our fault.

At our next meeting, Julie suggested that dead birds become our next focus. We think, she said, looking at everything besides me, we're in the middle of the story, but we're not. We're jumping from one end to another, never believing that one day, one day, there'll be no more stories to run *to*.

Mags pressed her pen against her notebook, then dropped it.

Well, I said, in an attempt to crack the film of devastation that had settled over the group, *I* was into dead birds before they were famous.

Everyone laughed, apart from Julie, who, looking at me for the first time since we'd fucked in reality, said, you could've got an article in the *Guardian* if you'd had more initiative.

By the time we sourced our bird suits and scheduled a Saturday to lie down in them, you had to scroll for at least seven minutes before you saw a dead bird on the internet. This wasn't because they'd stopped falling out of the sky; it was because we'd got used to it. Now, the men who sold phone cases and umbrellas in the street, also sold doormats, so no one had to trample feathers into their homes.

We lay in the middle of the pedestrianised shopping street where previously we had circled. I had imagined people would step on or trip over us; that they would kick us or spit at us; that, at the very least, they'd film us on their phones. In all of these scenarios, Julie and I transcended this adversity, along with our personal differences, through a complex language of hand-squeezing. But the Saturday shoppers stepped around us in the same way they stepped around the actual dead birds: as if they'd been doing it forever. I worried that human progress consisted only of finding new ways of not-seeing what it pained us to see. I worried that nothing meant anything. I worried that worrying I wasn't real because no one was looking at me meant that I really wasn't real.

I considered lying there, staring up at the sky not-staring at me; I did consider it.

But my phone buzzed and although I knew it would not give me any of the things it promised, I reached for it.

Then something smacked against my chest.

My left boob went numb. The thing was small and wet. Someone, somewhere, screamed. It was a superficial scream; a scream which believed that things would soon go back to normal; a scream which, as the numbness gave way to stinging and the stinging spread from my left boob to my right, was absorbed into the background traffic of 'Hey Jude' and strangers' footsteps. A hand squeezed my hand, but I didn't see who it belonged to because my eyes were already shut. That was some time ago. I've found no reason to reopen them—yet.

The Real Meaning of Coffee

W HEN ESTHER ASKED Molly for coffee, Molly
wanted to ask Esther if by *coffee* she meant talk for
maybe twenty minutes about the concentric brown hearts
that made up the unbearably earnest teenage barista's latte
art, and about why, seeing as almost no one in the UK
ordered lattes, only flat whites, no one called it flat-white
art, even though the answer—flat-white art did not exactly
roll off the tongue—was obvious; and whether, when the
word *tongue* produced a silence so loud that made it impossible to not look at or think about Esther's tongue and
what she might do with it besides destroy latte art, Esther
would also be thinking about Molly's tongue, and about
whether Molly was thinking about Esther's tongue; what
Molly wanted, to ask was, whether by *coffee* Esther meant
talking as a precursor or possibly a rehearsal for a fuck.
They had, after all, already had at least three conversations
about how difficult it was to know whether a date was a
date date or a friend date when you were a queer woman.
They had exchanged several silences which were, she was
pretty sure, tongueful. The problem was, she could never
be *sure* sure. The disappointment that would come with

Molly saying no, sorry, I don't like you that way, was, to the disappointment of going for a coffee only to find that it was only a coffee and would lead to many more only-a-coffees, what birth contractions were to period pain. That Molly felt the pain of both childhood and rejection despite never having experienced either was proof of how bad they were.

When Esther asked Molly for a coffee, Molly said, yes, I love coffee, and Esther smiled, she smiled with her mouth open, and Molly tried not to stare into the blackish pink space where her tongue probably was; it was almost as if the moment she'd just imagined might happen was already happening, only that it wasn't, because Molly's mouth was now making shapes, and the shapes were making sounds, and the sounds were meant to make words, and the words were meant to make meanings, and the meanings were meant to make—what? What was the point of it all, exactly?

I *said*, said Esther, does Thursday work? Her tongue disappeared behind the bright white light of her phone calendar.

Molly nodded. She was disappointed, not only that Molly had not immediately understood the real meaning of coffee, but that, in all the days and hours she'd spent (wasted?) imagining different varieties of disappointment, she'd failed to imagine this one.

Crime With No Culprit

Y OU ALWAYS RUN, never walk, often run whilst texting whilst listening to an audio book whilst voice-noting your mum whilst trying to not-think about that paper you're failing to write in the hope that the Thing it is missing will, from the depths of your subconscious, be revealed, though of course, the passive construction makes it difficult—as you constantly remind your students—to tell who is doing what to whom; you often say this whilst filling out the register or answering emails whilst pretending to fill out the register; the last time you did this, they all looked so shocked, you wondered whether your mouth had taken advantage of your brain's relative absence to say something, well—obscene.

'What did I just say?' You picked on a student who was brazenly scrolling her phone.

She hearted a photo of some carrots piled up in a bin, then looked up. 'That the passive voice dissimulates language's true power structures.'

Dissimulate was pretentious, but, hey, it could be worse, it could be so much worse.

Though why are you thinking about this as if it is

happening right now when it happened not yesterday nor the day before yesterday, but the day before the day before yesterday, about two hours before you fell asleep on the bus, only to be awoken by a sentence that was—particularly given it had woken you just in time for you to not-miss your stop—unarguably your paper's Thing? You really were woken *by* it, just as the one who was writing and not-sleeping and barely-eating and barely-washing and not-replying to your mum's reply to your voicenote—*darling, I'm sorry but I don't know what you're saying, I wish you'd just finish the sentences you start rather than abandon them as teenagers, wild, and unloved*—was barely you; it was more like they were being done to you; or for you; or *under* you; or all of the above, or none or some *or* which not even the best worst writers dared explore?

Now you have three thousand and twenty-six words, nine thousand and thirty-three characters, and they are all Thingless. Your heart is doing the sorts of things people's hearts do in the sorts of novels you warn your students neither to read nor to write. You probably just need to sleep, or to eat the chocolate chip cookies in the header photo of the recipe on which you are about to click, but which are already in your oven, and burnt. Terribly, terribly, burnt.

Exnamuh

T HE CONTROLLER TOLD you to sort the good apples from the bad. She told you that good apples were good apples and bad apples were soggy and brown. She told you it would be simple.

Alas, it was not. There were, it was true, a few apples whose badness was so advanced, they disintegrated into a cloud of mouldy brown mush when you attempted to pick them up, which begged the question: were they apples at all?

No. You thought ex-apple would be a more appropriate term. Though was it a tad offensive? Imagine if adults were called ex-children. Or middle-aged people ex-young people. Maybe you should call them an elppaxe. Yes. *Elppaxe*. It didn't even sound made up, well, no more than any word sounds made up if you say it over and over and over again.

But what you thought about the apples was irrelevant; what the apples thought about whether or not they were apples was irrelevant; apples did not think about whether or not they were apples or about whether they would pair well with whisky sours or with anything else; you should not be thinking anything else! You were literally the slowest apple sorter she had ever come across.

And how many *had* she come across? you asked, which made her scream exactly the sort of scream you imagined the elpaxes screaming when they heard what you had called them before you called them elpaxes.

You tried, then, to focus on the good apples—the ones with skin so firm and bright, it would not preserve them in this state of goodness forever.

Most of the apples, however, were neither good nor bad. From one side, they were pristine, but when you turned them over, you'd find a mighty worm hole, or a section of skin that was suspiciously soft, brown and/or flat. It was as if parts of the apple were still fully apple, whereas others had had enough. Consigning them to the 'bad' box felt like telling people they might as well die now seeing as they were bound to die sooner or later.

For this reason—and also because you could not help yourself from eating the unambiguously good—your boxes remained empty.

You understand that you're paid by weight? The Controller said. She twisted her neck towards the other side of the orchard, where the other sorters were lugging heavy boxes of good and bad towards the pulping machine.

This. She thrust an apple under your nose. Good? She said. Or bad?

Umm … well, that tiny patch there looks quite bad, that patch looks like it might be about to go bad, and that—

It's fine. She threw it into the 'good' box.

Fine, you said, has very different connotations from *good*.

She did a thing with her face that felt very much like a

slap. You'd have liked to asked how she did it—being able to slap people without actually touching them is a life skill you've been coveting for some time—but your *don't-be-an-idiot* voice, which had been hiding who knows where this whole time, told you not to. Then she left and the voice told you that if you wanted to be a 'you' who walked out of this orchard in the possession of more money than in which you'd entered, you'd have to sort the apples.

Well, you obeyed it. You filled one box of 'goods' and another of 'bads'.

See, she laughed, that wasn't so difficult, was it?

You carried the boxes towards the juicer.

A woman who informed you she was currently in the Top Five juicers, wrinkled her nose. Is that all?

She switched on the pulper.

Go on.

You raised my box over the pulper's dark mouth, through which you could see its blades, already turning, hungry for more than the straggles of skin that remained from its last feed. But some voice in you, a different voice, one you wouldn't dare name, said: no. Said: sorting is the worst sort of violence. Your don't-be-an-idiot voice replied: *don't be an idiot*. You shifted the box from one hand to the other, not knowing which to trust.

What's wrong with you?

She doesn't speak English.

She does, she just doesn't speak.

She's been speaking to the apples!

No, she's been eating them.

We're not allowed to eat them!

Are you sure she's a *she*?

The other sorters, their voices and their bodies, pressed your body, and all its voices, towards the pulper. Your head was now hanging over that hungry mouth, the blades so close, they were spitting pieces of ex-ex-ex- apple up into your face. You thought: this must be it. Your passage from humanity to whatever is a human's next or ex or exnamuh.

It wasn't, though. The Controller yanked you away from the blade just in time. You almost caused an insurance claim that would've bankrupted the whole orchard?

After trying and failing to imagine the trees surrendering their mortgages and their grannies' jewels to the bank, you left.

You took the boxes of neither-goods-nor-bads in lieu of pay, though you've eaten none of them yet; you can't even think about your teeth meeting their skins without hearing that scream. You hear it almost all of the time. As if an apple, or a human, or some other creature, is passing from itself to whatever is outside of the self—now. And now. And now.

And now.

Clunky

I COULD TELL you about free radicals: they are atoms which, lacking electrons from their outer shells—though why these electrons departed their hosts, or how, I do not know; the only article that looked likely to explain this was behind a forty-dollar pay wall—manically bump into other atoms in the hope that they'll find some unfree conservative to whom they might bond and therefore complete themselves. 'Unfree conservative' of course my word; the eighteen free articles I've read on the topic used the term 'stable.' 'Hope' is also mine, and I was going to say that the articles did not imbue the atoms with any sort of intentionality or cognition, but then I clicked onto one of the 17 tabs that is open in the window behind the one I'm writing in, which is the Notes app btw, in case you're wondering, which you won't be, you are out there probably doing something incredibly stable, like repotting your plants or pre-soaking chickpeas for tomorrow's tea, and thus have no idea that I am wearing the same pair of pyjamas I wore yesterday and the day before, though they aren't actually pyjamas, I don't own any actual pyjamas, I could open a new tab and buy some right now, but somehow I can't, because the thing about me is I am missing something that is not quite physical; what it is, I can't tell you, hence I am clunking through this metaphor, which is no doubt as scientifically inaccurate as it is artistically crude because I didn't read even half of those eighteen free articles, I sort of skimmed them, then got embroiled in a What's App group chat re did its 9 members enjoy Secondary School, and although I have not thought about Secondary School for a long time, in fact, probably not since that day we stayed up all night talking about it, suddenly reading and responding to the chat's 49 messages felt like the thing I needed to be doing most of all. But by the time I'd worked out what I wanted to type into the chat box, there were another 71 messages, mostly the laugh-crying emojis, the first few of which were reactions to a video of a pig and a chicken appearing to dance with one another; the next, to a TikTok video of an eighteen-year-old explaining how lame it was that millennials still used the laugh-crying emoji instead of okgnBEktenlDNGqo3ihNDF, which was apparently the cool new way to express the absurdity of existence that is, one might say, the one stable feature at comedy's core.

By the end of that last sentence, I was certain that my bladder was about to burst; I dashed down to the bathroom but one of my seven housemates was showering, and although I could have dashed down another flight of stairs and through the garden and across the green at the back of the garden to the gap between the sheds in the Community Garden that never contains any community or anyone at all, and where I thus might therefore relieve my bladder,

I did not; the part that was about to burst was the one I am still trying to speak from, though why, I don't know, it doesn't have a mouth and no quantity of clunking will change that, but never mind, what I meant to say was that I first saw the words 'free radical' at the bottom of a Very Serious *Guardian* article—though what that was about, I no longer remember, I just have to hope that a few electrons' worth of seriousness have by now filled whatever gaps exist in whatever sorts of atoms exist inside me, though can a gap exist when it is the opposite of existence, I don't know, ffs, why is my mind like those cheap laces you used to buy from the market that would immediately fray?—and what I thought, no, what *happened*, was that those words made the memory of that march, I think it was to Stop the War or Cancel Tuition Fees or something from the time before smartphones, from before the slew of other Terrible Things that now make the war and tuition fees seem marginally less terrible, anyway, the sight of words, shimmering between 'lose 10 lb of belly flab in 10 days' and '19 household objects that are actually cakes', sort of rubbed the memory of it loose from whatever atoms of molecules it had been clinging to all these years and suddenly, your shoulder was brushing against mine and man, how I wanted to lean over and kiss the mouth that was talking about how much better the world might would could be if only people got it into their dumb heads that there was more to life than buying things and laughing at things, and then someone started to push a lot of other people, and someone else told them to stop, and now everyone was crashing into everyone else and the thought came that I might die but that I'd be closer to you than I'd ever been so I wouldn't mind and that, *that*, is what I mean when I say I miss you, which is not what the me who sat down to write this meant to say, at all.

Everything You Need & More>

MEH
***

I've been jarring two days a week for three months now, which is two weeks after what my favourite Youtuber and my second-favourite *Guardian* columnist and even my third-favourite punk band lead singer said was the point at which your manual said customers could expect to feel significant cognitive and spiritual change, but my thoughts still taste like yesterday's cigarettes—and I'm not even a smoker.

Edit: I just posted a draft of this review to my Stories and my flatmate said I should read the manual myself rather than relying on randos off the internet to read it for me—which is exactly the sort of know-it-all comment that I hoped the jar might help me escape from, and anyway, it's not like I can just sit around all day reading random manuals, I've got a life to lead, and even, if, say, I did somehow find the time—I can literally hear my flatmate pointing out that I could've read it in the time I've been writing this—cba.

IF MY BRAIN IS IN ITS JAR AND THE JAR IS IN MY GARAGE AND MY BODY IS IN THE BASEMENT, WHICH IS WHERE MY COMPUTER IS, WHO OR WHAT IS THE 'I' THAT IS NOW WRITING?
****

It's not in your FAQs.

IF THIS IS WHAT THE WORLD IS COMING TO, I WANT ANOTHER ONE
*

Worst experience of my life. By 'worst' I mean it wasn't an experience. I mean it was an experience, but not of life. I don't know what things mean anymore. The grey fluff that has for years mysteriously appeared in my belly-button, now appears under my armpits. My nose won't stop dripping. My toes are too hot and too cold and whenever I look at them, I think about the sausages in the butcher's that was around the corner from the house where I grew up, though it feels more like the sausages are thinking about me, and now I can't eat them, not even my wife's homemade ones, which I formerly loved.

My body was much easier, before.

Nevertheless, it was too hard, and if I thought about it, I only thought about how much Bigger my thoughts would be were they freed from it. My wife and I don't exchange anniversary gifts; instead, we each transfer £100 into the other's private account, then buy ourselves exactly what we want. Well, I've never felt as close to that target as I did when I unwrapped the Perfecto Brain Jar (VI.9).

I should point out here, that I followed the brain-preparation schedule to the letter. In fact, to the full stop.

The first few seconds: sublime—absolutely sublime.

Then, Winston. Winston is our cat. He has dexterous paws; he jumped up into the windowsill where I'd placed the jar, and, within seconds, the lid was off. She (we named her before discovering her sex, though she is still the most macho cat I've come across, despite her lack of balls) began to swipe at my brain the way she used to swipe at the goldfish, and all I/it/the brain wanted, was to cry. Not, however, because it/I feared dying between Winston's jaws; it was that I spied, a few feet behind Winston's swishing tail, the body. It was standing between the bed and the door to the ensuite bathroom. I didn't know whether it was mine. My wife was sitting on the bed. She was talking with her mouth and her hands and, occasionally, her shoulders. She was talking as if my 'I' and my brain were exactly where they were supposed to be. She didn't—and here, I must hand it to you—suspect a thing. I've always thought of myself as a solid person, and not just because my underpants size is XXXL; my wife would occasionally whisper things late at night along the lines of: I don't know what it's all for, who are we really, etc, etc and I would remind her she was a real person, not a character in a pretentious French novel.

Now, however. I, I mean my brain, I mean—I don't know what I mean, well, from this perspective for which there is no word, or if there is, I'm too imbecilic to find it, maybe I should've paid more attention in French. At any rate, from here, I mean there, I mean—compared to the walls and the bed and curtains and the window and the patch of grass and mud that in one hundred and seventy-seven mortgage payments time, would be ours, not to forget the sky, which would never be ours, though I'd read that some billionaires were working out ways to make it theirs, and the clouds, which would already have moved to another patch of sky by the time I'd thought the word 'clouds', ditto the aeroplane, if there was an aeroplane, though I doubt there was as we do not, thank god, live on a flight path, though that is not to say that planes never veer from their paths, because they do, and often, unless they are not planes but flying saucers disguised as planes, but that is too large of a veer from any reasonable path for me, which was—what? Ah yes. The body. It was so—small. It reminded me of that godforsaken toy my son used to call a water willy. He was forever juggling it from one hand to another. If we told him to stop, he'd whack it against the edge of the table; after two or three whacks it would invariably burst, submerging our dinners in its soapy green innards. The body was bigger than the water willy, but weaker, much weaker; I mean, what is skin compared to plastic: it is dying all the time, but plastic never dies, the water willy will outlive me and my son and his son, if he has one, though maybe, by then, children will be banned? It, the body, life, death, the sky, etc, was a disaster. The desire to cry and the inability to do so transformed my brain into a zone of pain such as I've never known. So, as per your instructions (which, even for someone such as myself who

relishes a crisp, clear chain of command, were far too long),
I imagined bumping the brain against the big red button
on the bottom of the jar, but the brain did not move as I'd
imagined, but to the side, then to the other side, then up,
up, towards—but Winston's paw wasn't there anymore.
Nor was Winston. I don't know where he'd gone. As soon
as I began to ponder this, forgetting completely the button,
the tears, the etc—boom. I/the brain, bumped it.

Then I was viewing my wife from an angle that must've
been that other jar, I mean, my skull.

'What's wrong?' she asked. She was starting to look
as if she did, after all, suspect me of not being where she
thought I was.

I shook my head.

'You look a bit constipated.'

I told her that was impossible; it wasn't forty minutes
since I'd emptied my bowels. Then I told her some other
things, I don't remember what; all I remember is that there
were holes in them, the words, I mean; the things they
were meant to be about just fell through them. Winston
rubbed against my calf and when I looked down she was
scowling up at me.

'Where did that vase come from?'

The jar. She was talking about the jar.

I shrugged.

'Did you buy it?'

I nodded.

'Then how can you not know?'

Again, I shrugged.

She scowled at me in the way Winston was already
scowling at me.

'It's ugly,' she said, eventually, and I could neither agree nor disagree.

I still can't cry.

I WANTED TO RATE THIS BOTH ONE AND FIVE STARS BUT THE COMPUTER SAID NO

***

You know when it's hot and your thighs rub and rub and the skin goes red then blisters then pops then peels off? Well, it's like that. The jar. The fucking jar. It chafes your brain, only, getting your brain out of the jar makes it even worse, and it won't pop, it just blisters and swells and you grab your skull and people say why are you grabbing your skull and you don't say, because I bought this dumb jar on the internet whilst drunk and by the time it arrived, I was horrifically hungover I thought oh wow for once I did a clever thing whilst drunk.

At first, it was perfect. Just—perfect. Or should I say perfectO?? Haha. No hangover, no worries, no hopes, no dreams, no hunger, no thirst, no pain, no pleasure, no things, no nothing.   Then . . . I don't know. I'm like this with relationships, jobs, breakfast cereals, shoes, everything: one moment, I'm living my best life, telling everyone how great it is, etc, etc; the next—doom. My therapist says it's that I am always cutting and snipping myself into a ton of distractible pieces like those of the jigsaw puzzles I mixed up whilst trying to do them whilst watching a mindfulness meditation and that new comedy series set in a factory where they make eternal life, except that the people who work there don't get it, they actually die earlier as a result, but yes, anyway, I bumped myself

(or should I say brain? neither one feels right) against the
jar and then I was back in my body, except that my body
was not my body because my brain is still in that jar and
yes, I know this is impossible, the jar is all still present
and correctly brainless and gathering dust on the kitchen
counter but goddamit there is a chafing there is this
feeling   like everything in me is swelling blooming-
bursting into everything else but why won't it when will it
will it never—pop?

LIES !!!!!!
*****

You say: '*Every jar is made to your intellect's bespoke meas-
urements, as indicated in the 'jar preparation kit.*' Well, it's
lies! All! Lies! And no, before you suggest, a la your online
helpbot, Jessica, that I simply misread! the instructions! I
did not!!! My intellect is, according to your own specifica-
tions, in the top percentile for heft! And length! So tell me!
Please? Why, then, it got stuck? For days. Days and days.
You may laugh; you will not be the first (that would be my!
wife!!?). But those were dark days, I tell you. Dark! Days!
And my brain hasn't been the same since. Exclamation
marks, for example! I never! used them! before. So why?
now?! Please, will a human! reply? Thank you, sir! And if
you're a madam, please don't tell me off for sirring you first!

IF THERE'S A GOD GENDER, THIS MUST BE IT
*****

The first time, I was like: take it or leave it. Then I sort of
forgot about it. Then my housemate used the jar to make
some kombucha, only, it was raspberry flavoured, I was

bored and I'd run out of weed and I read this subreddit about jarring on shrooms and I wished I had some shrooms but I didn't and then there was a tickling in my chest sort of like there was a cockroach trapped in there, which actually was a thing that happened the last time I shroomed, and then I wasn't sad I didn't have them anymore, and so stuck those stupid electrodes to my forehead and pressed that big red button and—MANOHBOHOHGOD. The high, the trip, the low, it was—incredible. I'm not going to give you one of those trip reports; they're corny. My flatmates are like: you need to go to work, you've not washed the dishes or your hair or your armpits for like three years, you kind of resemble a prehistoric pond creature and we did not sign up to live with a fake prehistoric pond creature, blah, blah. I don't care, I keep telling them that if they'd just try it, they wouldn't care, either. But do they listen? Does anyone ever listen? Do they hell.

YOU STOLE MY GIRLFRIEND
*

You state, in the safety guidance, that one's brain should not be jarred for more than one week out of every four; that every jar contains a built-in eject function for anyone who dares to approach this limit. You fail, however, to set a limit on the number of jars a person can buy. My girlfriend, for example, has fourteen. When she reaches the limit on one, she simply switches to another, and so on and so forth; when I talk to her, she isn't there. Of course, she denies this: 'I've not used in months,' 'all my jars are broken,' etc—you'll only have to scroll through a few of the JarAddictsSupportForum to run through the classic excuses. My friends think I should dump her. The problem is she, I mean the temporary motor that keeps her looking and acting like her when her brain is elsewhere, is clever. 'I'm here, I'm me,' she'll say, and she'll cry, 'It's just that you can't see me, or maybe you can, but you don't want to, you're fixated on this idea that there's another me out there, a real one, a better one, and that makes me feel like I'm not enough,' and although I'd just read about an almost identical speech in the Forum, some part of me that is a long way from my brain will get very soft. I'll apologise. Then she'll tell me it's fine, she was overreacting, it's probably that she was about to come on her period. Ah yes, I'll say, I *did* wonder. Then she'll accuse me of being a misogynist, and I'll deny, and so on and so forth, and this is so much like the sort of *we* we used to do before I, heaven forgive me, bought her v.13 for her birthday—and only because she was always complaining that she hated her body, etc—that I almost forget she isn't really her. I would've put zero stars in the review if there had been that option, but there wasn't.

YOU DON'T KNOW YOU'VE BEEN BORN
*****

What is wrong with you people? Do you know that most humans throughout history would have KILLED for an opportunity to escape their stupid bodies for even a second? Why do you think they used to get drunk all the time?! Gratitude, gratitude, ffs.

SUGGESTION BOX
***

I notice that you incorporated, into your latest update, my

suggestion to include a 'Find My Body' function. (Hope you enjoyed my anecdote re when my body absconded from my sister's wedding as much as I didn't!?) The thing is, I'm not sure it works, e.g. the body it 'found' was not mine, at least, I thought it wasn't, but when I said this out loud, my loved ones looked at me as if I was even madder than when I/my body/the body absconded from said wedding, and so I said no more, and eventually I, too, began to wonder whether this had been my body all along. It was simply that my time in the jar—and I'm not an addict; I almost always terminate my jar-dom at least a day before the limit; I still hold down three different jobs and I'm vice president of my local air hockey team and we are about to compete at the regional championships and I don't want to jinx it but I'm pretty sure we're going to win—had radically altered the relationship between me and it. *Radically.* So I think that next time—and your incorporation of my previous suggestions gives me hope that there's a human, at least as real as I am, reading this—you update the English language, paying particular attention to pronouns, also verbs, also nouns, also the spaces between them, also the symbols used to regulate such spaces, such as commas, exclamation marks, and full stops.

TRUE LOVE
*****

I just want to say thank you. I am a mother of four (five if you count my husband, six if you count the dog my husband insisted that our youngest insist we have, and which I, of course, look after, seven if you count the children from my husband's first and second marriages—he got started young!—who use our house as a refuge from their supposedly "grown-up" lives) and the time when my brain is jarred is the only time I can think. I don't think anything particularly clever or interesting; mostly, I just look out at the garden. I look at the leaves' colours, which are so vivid and various; I look for ages and ages and I am only still starting to see them. Certain people's faces used to make me feel this way; I'd look; I'd stare; I'd know it was rude to stare, but I couldn't help it: their particular arrangement of eyes, nose, mouth, etc, etc, was a mystery I would never unravel, not that I wanted to. No, I felt the way maybe our cat feels when it plays with a ball of string. My body, meanwhile, continues to do all the things all its children and semi-children pester it to do. Do any of them notice its brainlessness? No, they do not. They do, however, notice my disorientation upon my brain's return. MUM, they'll yell, I SAID, where's my swimming stuff??! They have no idea where I've been, and some days this makes my stomach zing in the way it used to zing in that period, about which I will say no more, when I did sometimes, yes, I will admit it, steal a thing or two from shops (only small things, only big shops). Other days, I just want to cry. I want someone to look at me the way I look at the leaves.

See All Buying Options >
Add to Wish List >
Add to Basket >
Buy Now >
Bye, Now

Thruple

THERE ARE THREE people in this relationship: me, her and that other person—the one who, by fucking and reading our books instead of fucking and getting too drunk to fuck and watching other people watch TV together and [insert mundane-couple activity of your choice here], we are constantly hoping to meet.

Almost everything we do—fucking, not-fucking, reading our books instead of fucking, watching other people watch TV instead of fucking, etc—we do with the hope of meeting the third—though in many ways, first—person in our relationship.

Once, when we each orgasmed twenty-four times in a twenty-four period, we got close, very close. She claimed that the third person was made of lightning: our bedroom was bisected by seams of light so bright she insisted on wearing sunglasses. I told her she looked like a dick; she told me that she didn't think the third person was meant to be seen: the light was now burning her brain. She could *literally* feel it sizzling. This was, we would later find out, the beginning of a four-day migraine.

Of course, the third person could go at any time. I know

it; she knows it; we are both almost certain that they know that we know it; yet, in an effort to disrupt, or at least paper over this chain of knowing, we have named them Ogog. We do not strain towards them as we used to—five is now more orgasms than either of us can handle—but we do always serve them a smallish portion of whatever we are eating. We bought them a special plate, hand-kilned, and a shade of turquoise that makes me smack my lips every time I look at it, although this irritates her so much that I do my best not to look at it (although my best isn't very good given that telling myself not to look at it only makes me look longer at it). They eat whatever we give them, though no matter how many times we resolve that *this* time, we will not by distracted by thoughts or talk or talk of thoughts or talk about other people's thoughts on the internet or talk about other people's thoughts about other other people's thoughts on the internet dubbed through cartoon cats, we have not witnessed the moment of ingestion—yet.

That is not to say that our life is without its problems; a life without problems is not really a life, is it? (Is it?). Ogog inflicts us with moods, Moods, and, if things are really bad, MOODS. Their persistent shunning of the visual realm makes it easy for us to blame the other for their appearance, a process which, paradoxically, fills our bodies with Moods which, although not quite as big or as bad as Ogog's, are unarguably ours.

Ogog's moods also function as a divide and rule policy: they afflict them on one of us but not the other. The Afflicted will greet the Unafflicted's pleadings to get out of bed and go to that party with scorn: never, ever, *ever* will she get out of bed. OK, she might, quite soon, when she needs to empty her bladder, get out of bed, but she will absolutely never *ever* go to a party. The Unafflicted will take Deep Breaths. She will try to remember the last time *she* was Afflicted; how certain she'd been that the affliction was all everything would ever be, forever. But when she says something to this effect, the Afflicted huffs and rolls her eyes at such an angle that the Unafflicted says, *oh for fuck's sake, can't you get yourself out of it?*

If we are lucky, the MOOD quickly abates. But if it carries on, and on and on and on and on, the Unafflicted starts to wonder whether we'd be better off just the two of us, and it is always at this point that it, mysteriously or not mysteriously—draw your own conclusions, if conclusions are what you need to draw—ends.

Let's go for dinner! Somewhere special! says the one who is No-Longer Afflicted, already googling restaurants.

We book a table for three, and when the waiter asks if we're ready to order, we say yes, and when he asks, his eyes hovering in the seat between us—Ogog always sits in the middle—whether we're waiting for anyone, we say no. *We have everyone here that we need.* Then we tell him to hurry up and pour our wine, making sure, of course, that Ogog's glass is the fullest.

Terms and Conditions

Vee found me in the toilets of Leeds' fanciest pasta restaurant.

I was washing my hands, she asked what was wrong, I said nothing, she said, so why don't you go back to your friends, I said, I would be if you weren't asking me this, she said, you want to cry, I said I never cried, she said that was fucked up, I said that what was fucked up was that even when I was having a good time in life, and good was the sort of time I was having now, I felt as if it was all a distraction from my real purpose, my real home.

The friends in the restaurant were my very best friends. I told them that I told them everything. I didn't, though. I'd never told them what I'd just told Vee, not even after my mouth was numbed by drugs. I'd tried, once or twice, but only a few sentences in, they began to look at me like I was the un-instagrammable sort of mad, so I stopped.

Vee didn't judge me; I knew it as I was speaking, and I knew it in the silence that followed.

So let go, she said. Let go of time.

How, I asked.

She rolled her eyes. Stop filling yourself up with pasta.

But I love pasta.

I really did; I was the one who'd instigated 'Pasta Tuesday' on the last week of every month. I ate more than whoever I was eating with. I'd never been on a diet.

That's not you, she said, it's your greed, and it's getting in the way of your purpose.

She leaned in, as if to kiss me, then pulled away. Resist it, she said, resist. Then she walked back into the restaurant, and although I walked only half a metre behind, I couldn't see her when I sat back down.

You took your time, said Paula, were you voicenoting someone? Or scrolling Instagram? What's your guiltiest scroll? And don't say cat videos. We all know we all look at worse things than cat videos.

I couldn't focus on her words. I kept twisting around. I wanted to see her again. I wanted to know how I knew her name, even though she'd never told me it.

I know, said Maisie, it's obvious. She's staring at that waitress. She fancies her.

Classic Alex behaviour, said Paula, and everyone laughed.

This sort of ribbing was the bread and butter of our friendship, but it filled me with as much shame as the idea of actually putting bread and butter into my body. I didn't finish my pasta. I didn't laugh or explain myself when Paula asked why I hadn't finished my pasta. Vee's voice was still ringing through my ears, reminding me how much better she knew me, and how much better I'd know myself once I followed her advice.

In the days that followed, I hoped to see her again, but I

didn't, not in the way I'd seen her in that bathroom. That didn't matter, though, because on the fourth day of eating about half as much as I'd eaten before I met her, I began to hear her voice. *Good*, she said, *but not good enough. You are still letting your greed get the better of you. That slice of bread with your salad, for example. Was it really necessary?*

The more I listened, the more ideas she shared. She had so many ideas! Like shaking my legs under my desk and walking to the printer that was furthest away from my desk and going to the gym at lunch rather than listening to the colleague I didn't even like speculate on whether or not she would hook up with the PR officer (she wouldn't; he was clearly gay). When she spoke, I felt as if I was floating out of my desk or my chair or wherever my body was(n't) and into the other place, the one I was meant to be. It was beautiful there. Beautiful and easy, because my purpose, my one and only purpose, was to please her.

The downside was that when you were up there, it was hard to understand what was happening, down here, on earth. For example, I did a mailmerge inviting my company's key stakeholders to an event on the 69th of July. I failed to notice a mistake on an invoice that cost my company a thousand pounds. I often took the train in the wrong direction, I put ice cream in the cupboard and biscuits in the freezer, I forgot my own pin code, I accidentally poured boiling water all over my hand instead of into the hot water bottle. I didn't eat the ice cream or the biscuits, and not only because I'd stored them in the wrong places; I didn't even want to eat them: food, like sex, like dating, like fancying people, now felt irrelevant.

When Paula told me she was pregnant, I said nothing

and when she said are you angry, I said no, and when she said why are you just sitting there like a stone, I said what, and she said nothing for so long that I thought she was going to cry. She didn't, though. She asked if I'd been listening. I said yes, she said, what did I just say, I said I don't know, she said so you weren't listening, you never listen anymore, it's like you're not there. Maisie's noticed, too. It's like you're no longer interested in anything outside yourself.

Before, such comments would have destroyed me. I mean, *destroyed*. Not anymore. Because Paula, like everyone else, was trapped in time, waiting, always waiting, for fulfilment. I, however, I was in the temporal equivalent of a motorway layby. Nothing and no one could touch me.

And we've noticed you've missed Pasta Tuesday, she said. We've missed you. We wondered . . . She glanced at my legs, which were still jiggling under the table, if you are OK.

I'm fine, I said, I've just been busy. I'll come next week, I said, even though Vee was hissing at me, she didn't like me to spend time with other people, especially not when food was involved, I promise.

Ok, said Vee, when Paula was gone, *it's probably better that you go, since they seem quite suspicious, but you will have to meet the terms and conditions...*

And herein lay the other problem: it was impossible to meet them. It was impossible to satisfy her, no matter how closely I followed the rules. If she said I could have soup for lunch, she'd insist, two spoons in, that I could only eat half, and only if I skipped my three plain almonds that afternoon, and if I did all that, she'd say, yes, but you've been thinking about food all this time, you've been thinking about food because you are so fucking greedy. You're the greediest person that ever lived why can't you rise up over your hunger and into the realm of ultimate philosophical truth? Why can't you be like Simone Weil?

Somehow, I dragged my body to Pasta Tuesday. I made it look as if I was looking at the menu and listening to the sounds coming out of Paula's and Maisie's mouths. But I wasn't, my vision was blurred, my ears seemed to amplify the screech of strangers' knives and forks but mute my friends' voices. My body was there, but my I, my soul, or whatever you want to call the part of you that won't fit in your body, not completely, it was in the lay-by. It was in the lay-by even though it didn't want to be, only, it lacked the energy to stand up, to try the emergency pay phone, to wave its arms and shout for help.

When the waitress returned to take our orders, I froze. I wished I would pass out and wake up in a better place. I didn't, though. I just sat there, feeling more and more stupid and anxious and trapped.

For god's sake, said Maisie, it's not rocket science.

But that's exactly how it feels, I wanted to say. Exactly.

How about the mushroom tagliatelle, Paula said in the too-soft voice she used with her cockapoo that was as stupid as it was pretty. You love that.

No you don't, you don't, it's not you, it's just your greed, you're the greediest human that ever lived you must try harder.

Ok, I said, sure.

Then Paula began to talk about her morning sickness and how it never came in the morning but at random times or random days and Maisie began to talk about how her hangovers were the same like she would wake up thinking she'd gotten away with it and then when she was halfway through what would've been a very nice meal she'd have to run to the bathroom and throw up, she'd been doing that a lot with Dan, they had great sex and drank too much.

They talked and I watched. They were in time, rushing through it, grabbing at whatever and whoever came their way. They were alive, and I, I was in the layby, shaking my legs up and down, down and up.

Fuck's sake, can you stop that, said Maisie, when the pasta arrived.

Paula shot her a look that made me sure they'd discussed me when I wasn't there. Are you feeling anxious?

I nodded. I said it had been stressful at work. But when they asked for details, I couldn't give any, I could think of nothing besides the pasta and how I might pick out the mushrooms without them noticing.

You're not on a diet, are you? Maisie sounded suspicious. We prided ourselves on not being *those* sorts of women.

No.

Then why won't you eat your pasta?

I ate so much birthday cake in the office today, I lied.

You've lost weight.

Only a few pounds.

Vee said that, not me, and it was Vee, believe it or not, who forced a few spoonfuls of pasta into my mouth, even after my shrunken stomach was full. *If they find out about me, they'll want to separate us*, she said. *Eat more now so that you can eat less later. Play the long game.*

The next time I saw Paula was at Maisie's barbecue. I wanted her to ask, again, about food. I had rehearsed a million better answers than the one I'd given at the pasta restaurant; I'd imagined telling her how the less I ate, the greedier she made me feel, how I now found it difficult to distinguish her voice from my own. But she didn't, she just asked about work and about dating and about life and when I had nothing to say about any of it because I was worrying about how much of the barbecue food Vee would let me eat, she went and talked to a friend of Maisie's girlfriend I knew she found incredibly boring and when she didn't come back, Vee said it was because I was even more boring and so, without telling anyone, I left.

I walked all the way home, stopping only for a 'no bread sandwich', a concept past-me loved to ridicule. When I checked my phone, I had loads of missed calls from Paula. Why didn't you say goodbye? Love you, miss you, she texted. Then there was a text from Maisie instructing me to come back, things had taken a turn towards the sesh.

You can go, said Vee, but you must stick to drugs, not booze, you must get so fucked that it won't matter that you won't be able to exercise tomorrow since you also won't be able to eat anything.

I followed her advice to the letter. About fifteen keys in, a miracle occurred: she shut up. For the first time in months, I heard silence, and a few more hours and keys later, I told Maisie some of the things I'd imagined telling Paula.

I knew it, she said. I knew you had an eating disorder, but I guess I was in denial because I didn't want you to have one, not you, you always seemed to love food.

Oh no, I said, it's not *that* bad. I mean, I can stop anytime I want, and it's not like I want to be thin or anything, it's just this sense of purpose, it's so strong.

Then she said a lot of words, many of which were accompanied by incredibly earnest and sweaty hand-squeezes. When they were over, I agreed. I agreed that I needed to stop. I needed to resist her. I needed to eat.

The next day, I threw up for twelve hours straight.

The day after that, my stomach was so small, that eating even a few rice cakes felt like too much. Vee, of course, was delighted. Absolutely delighted, and so was I, until I walked to Sainsbury's. It was a short walk, very short and very flat, and I almost passed out. I sat down on a bench that was usually occupied by old people. My phone buzzed. *Just found this, such a lovey shot.* Paula had whatsapped me a photo from the night I first met Vee. I was talking to Maisie, my mouth open, lips smeared with sauce—it made me feel homesick. It made me wonder whether that life had been my real life, and this, whatever I was doing with Vee, was the distraction.

Don't be ridiculous, Vee, said, *you weren't happy then, you've got to keep going, you've got to try harder, you're almost there.*

There is no *there*, I said, out loud, and a man walked by but he didn't look at me like I was mad, he didn't hear me, his ears, like almost everyone else's, were stuffed with headphones.

There's no lay-by, I said, or if there is, it's shit in the way diet bread is shit, it never fills you up.

She had a lot to say about that, but I didn't listen. I practically skipped to the supermarket. I was going to buy bagels, cream cakes, pizza . . . All the things she'd forbidden. I *was*. Except that I really didn't feel so bad anymore. I felt really energetic! I stared at the bagels for forty-five minutes, before buying what I always bought: fruit and vegetables and rice cakes.

This happened every day for the next year.

Every day, the same non-day, same non-time in the nonexistent lay by.

I wished someone would save me, but every time they tried—Maisie kept offering to eat with me, to come to the supermarket with me, to the doctor—I told them I was fine. In the end, I had to save myself, only, it didn't feel like saving, it felt like losing, like losing the game, the purpose, the point, the safety, I didn't know why I was doing it, I didn't want to do it, it was more that I didn't want to not-live in the not-lay-by anymore, I didn't want to not-live.

We still go for Pasta Tuesday: me, Maisie, Paula, and Paula's baby, Ro. I order either the mushroom tagliatelle or the special, always with extra Parmesan. I talk of my life, which I'm in now, I am really in it, and it's really real, I am really licking the sauce off my plate. Sometimes they say things like: I'm so glad to have you back. I'm so glad you recovered.

I smile, I nod, I do not disagree.

What I do not say is that she's lurking in the window. Your jeans are too tight, she says, even though they are so much bigger than the jeans you wore when you were with me.

Sometimes I give her the evil eye, I tell her to fuck off, I shift my position so that she's out of sight.

But often I don't. I look back. Because I know that no matter how much pasta I eat, I'll never stop hungering for the old hunger. Perhaps she was right: I am the greediest.

Your Cervical Cancer Screening Test Is Overdue

I F THIS WERE not a moment from their actual lives but a scene in a novel at Book Club, Julia would say it was over the top. *Implausible*, was another word she might use; she might even purse her lips, frown at her wine glass in that way which made even Caroline and Helen shut up, then say that whilst she agreed that the climax—which is what this moment would be were it a scene in a novel; the ten or so pages a few dozen from the end when the author mercilessly broke open the narrative to reveal its ugly yet somehow still aesthetically-pleasing innards—was indeed 'devastating', and 'spell-binding,' and whatever other over-blown adjectives the cover pull-quotes claimed, it felt more like a misremembered version of someone else's idea of what these words might mean, rather than the author's own.

'Well,' Caroline would say, '*I* enjoyed it, and far more than that other book we read, the one you chose, you know, where nothing happened and the main character was this woman who just complained about everything even though her life was pretty good'.

'OKaayy,' Susan would reply, her tone unsubtly implying the opposite, 'let's pretend this book is real life. First, you get two wildly incompatible middle-aged women to get the hots for each other at an interminably boring book club—I mean a book club in a book, come on, how tacky—*then* they manage to conduct an affair for nine months, fucking in every room of each of their suburban houses without either of their husbands or teenage children noticing? It's the sort of thing such women would fantasise about at the tail-end of a boozy Friday night: they'd never actually do it; they're scared to get out of their boring little lives.'

There would be a silence, then Helen would crunch down the last of the Kettle Chips, and Julia would go on: 'But assuming all of this, somehow, happened, would they really plan to 'tell all' at the lunch that was supposed to be a celebration of their children going away to university? No, they'd talk about the couscous salad, and how it almost tasted like the one they'd had in Morocco, and what sorts of bedding they'd brought each child, and how they'd fit it in the car. Then the children would leave, and they'd fuck and they'd fuck until their love or lust or despair or whatever it was their bodies were trying to speed them towards or away from, dried up; after that, they'd resume their boring but somehow comfortable lives with their husbands.' Then she'd get that look, like she was doing a three-point turn in her mind. Susan could not do three-point turns, neither in her mind, nor in her car, nor anywhere else, and on more than one occasion the thought of Julia doing it had made her cum.

'Assuming,' hypothetical Julia went on, smiling as she pressed down on the accelerator on the car that would probably be the sort of metaphor the sort of writer of the sort of book about which she was talking would use for her mind, 'that they *did* opt for this melodramatic turn of events, would one woman's daughter, upon being asked, by the other woman, if she wouldn't mind passing her the couscous salad, say, yes, and then, your son raped me on the gifted-and-talented maths trip last year? Would that girl then collapse into a whole-body hysterics, just as her mother had, in that book club about the novel whose protagonist's brother dies in an ice-skating accident that they for some reason feel responsible for, which was the first time the other woman—the mother of the son who was meant to be here but was not, he was at his girlfriend's house, looking after her after her bladder operation, he was kind to her, he was kind to their dog, kind to his mother when no one else was, kind even to spiders and to slugs, and he still had this cute babyish fuzz up the back of his neck, none of which were words that ought to exist in the same sentence or even the same paragraph as —' But she couldn't say it, and this wasn't a novel and whatever point hypothetical Julia was about to make was now lost in real Julia, who was now rubbing Chloe's back and saying, 'Why didn't you tell me earlier?' and Chloe was rocking back and forth whilst clutching the couscous bowl, as if the couscous bowl might protect her from something, which was, come to think of it, the sort of thing a character in a novel might think; the difference, though, was that in a novel, it would mean something; but now was subsumed by a throbbing in her left temple and also her chest and potentially her stomach and her toes and it hurt and it meant as little as the invitation to a cervical screening test magnetted to the fridge and it hurt and it hurt and it was never not going to hurt.

Unless—Unless this was a draft. Yes. Maybe the author was about to realise that if Susan hadn't asked Chloe for the couscous; if she'd said, instead, 'Julia and I have something to tell you all,' then they'd already have said it, and the silence that now crackled between their bodies would be of an entirely different sort.

'I knew something was wrong, I knew it, but I pretended not to know it, and when I tried, you pushed me away.' But Susan was talking as if her daughter's words were a truth from which there was no going back to the future they'd been planning for so many months.

'Susan,' Julia whispered.

Susan looked up. 'What?'

'I – I – I don't even like couscous.'

The Big Squeeze

'THERE ARE TWO types of people in this world. Those that hate picking pimples and those that love it. And by *love* I mean, are *hot* for it.' Eli wiggled their eyebrows, as if they knew that my cock was now unbearably hard, and that, although said cock did not, as such, 'exist' , it was more real then everything that 'did'. 'Which are you?'

I said: 'I think you already know the answer.'

'I've a massive one in the middle of my back,' they said. 'Squeeze it for me?'

'*This*,' I said, as we joined the seemingly-endless queue for the Pump's one and only toilet, 'is what I mean when I say that I'm a gay boy trapped in a lesbian's body.'

'Lucky,' said Eli. 'I'm a lesbian trapped in a gay boy's body trapped in a bisexual ciswoman's body.'

'Too many traps?'

'It's comfy. Like wearing three layers of fishnet.'

'That makes me think of that documentary about the evils of the fishing industry.'

'You eat *fish*?' said the mulleted baby queer in front of us.

My phone pinged. *How's the Maybe-Date?! If it fizzles into another chaste 'what's your favourite vegan baking recipe' chat, wanna grab a drink later??!* It was Bea. My best friend since Primary School.

Out of this world, I texted back, then regretted it. What if I'd jinxed it?

'There's fish,' said an older femme who'd been staring at a Stop the Anti-Protest Bill poster for a very long time, 'and there's *fish*.'

Worse Leader had passed the Bill four months ago, and yet every time I saw that badly photocopied infinitive, my heart flapped around my chest, as if, maybe, just maybe, there was a chance things might still turn out differently.

'No one should shame anyone for what they eat,' shouted a queer who was wearing the same oversized cord shirt, rolled up jeans and stripy t-shirt as me.

I wondered whether, if the Council had accepted Pump's petition to take over the derelict brewery buildings that surrounded it and the queers of Leeds had, lo and behold, two or even *three* spaces to choose from, I'd be ripping off their dungarees about now.

'Wanna piss and do . . . other stuff . . . at mine?' they whispered, and I chased away the thought that we were telepathic.

The walk back to theirs was, thanks to the lack of buses and the profusion of tents, both of which were thanks to Worse Leader's cuts, lengthy. By the time they were unlocking their front door, we'd got the whole *lesbian* bit—relationship histories; star signs; attachment styles; childhood traumas; dungaree styles—out the way.

'Cup of tea? I've got this amazing loose-leaf Oolong.'

The lesbian in me was imagining us in six months'

123

time: three shiny cheese plants, homemade vegan 'feta' marinading in the fridge, Sunday debates re should we or should we not get a cat.

The gay boy, however, was in the ascendant: 'I want a cup of whatever is between your legs.'

Their left eyebrow arched. They stuck their fingers between my belt buckle and my skin, and pulled me up to their room.

What happened next: you might say it was sex. You might use words like *yes yes more more*. Your throat might be tangy with sweat.

But you would not see how, as their fist travelled up my vagina, a crack appeared in the bedroom wall, which their ex's ex had, for reasons they did not explain, persuaded them to paint mustard.

I screamed.

Their housemate threw something.

I closed my eyes, but the crack was right here, behind them. My eyeballs burned.

Then the not-sex, was, like all things, over. The wall was now crackless; healed, and purple. And Eli, Eli looked—*different*. Their eyebrows were dull and droopy. They handed me a cup of Oolong.

'When did you make that?'

Their dungarees were decidedly buckled. As were my jeans.

'Just now.'

'But didn't you just cum for the fifth time? And weren't your walls mustard?'

'If that's a joke, it's not funny.'

My heart felt like it was a fish trapped in the net of a conversation that a person I didn't know, and who didn't know why they were talking about fish, had started. 'You still haven't let me touch that pimple.'

They made a face. 'Why would I let you touch my pimples? That's gross.' They folded their legs up to their chest and cowered behind them.

I handed the Oolong back to them, then left—before they told me to.

Just as I was in danger of feeling seriously sorry for myself, a bus pulled up. It was new and shiny, of the sort I'd only ever seen in London. The driver stared at me. 'Getting on or not?'

I got on. I pulled out my bank card but there was no card reader, and when I asked how to pay, he screwed up his face and said, 'Where have you been, another planet?'

'Maybe,' I said.

'Well now you're here and no one is going to get *there* unless you bloody sit down.'

I sat down. The walls were adorned with posters in which the leader who I'd tried, without success, to persuade the older residents of the city to re-elect, smiled as if she'd won. I googled her name. Yep, she was the PM, though she was in the middle of reforming the political system so that it was less reliant on personalities, less centralised.

Which lesbian base are you at—long gazes, finger brushing, or shoulder bumping?!

Bea's text pinged right over the news story.

Weird.

Please come to PUMP rn and explain.

OK.

I hoped that by returning to the scene of what may or may not have been a crime, I'd find the detail that would make everything make sense.

Pump was no longer an ex-petrol station but a whole section of the city to which the ex-petrol station was a sort of gate house serving complimentary fluorescent shots and pills. Where previously there had been bins, rubble and concrete, there were now benches, tables, planters, fairy lights, and a giant swing over which several ghoulishly high adults were fighting. The brewery was foaming at the windows with lights, music, people, and plants, as was its roof. By the time Bea found me, my face was soggy with tears.

'Was it that bad?'

I shook my head. 'It—this—it's—' I'd never seen so many queers, just . . . being queer, in one spot. 'I—where are we?'

She tilted her head to the right and to the left, as if there was no angle from which she could see me clearly. 'We've been here at least twice a week since we were twenty-three. Are you . . . OK hun?'

'Yes. But also no. Also...' I squeezed her hand. It felt exactly as it had always felt, and nothing like a pimple, and for this I was glad. 'Let's go inside?'

The ground floor was a bar: big, but reassuringly chaotic, and soupy with the smell of deep-fried Seitan. On our way up to the second floor, we got extravagantly shooshed by a bow-tie queer; apparently there was an 'intergalactic medi-tation' in progress. On the third, a film-screening. On the fourth, there was a felt-tipped sign saying the rave would now be in the Other Building. Then the cold air smacked our cheeks; we were on the roof.

The sky, despite being in the middle of the city, was crowded with stars. People were dancing, talking, standing, sitting, in big groups, couples, threes, and alone. Someone was selling flapjacks for 50p each. Someone else was selling alcoholic kombucha —homemade! —from a freezer box. Behind all this, was a wall of ferns with a gap-come-door-way in the middle, and behind that came what was either extremely experimental music or sex noises.

'This is everything I hoped and dreamed of,' I said, my body moving towards the ferns without me telling it to. 'Except that it's nothing like anything I ever hoped and dreamed of, and that makes it so much better.'

Bea squeezed my shoulders. 'Something's . . . *happened* to you.'

'It's nothing.'

'Then why are you staring at The Beyond like it's the best thing since sliced bread?'

She meant the gap between the ferns. Before I could ask what she meant, she said she was going to check out Drag Towers, and was off.

I could say that I walked through the gap and landed on a huge fabric "lily pad," on which I proceeded to engage in group sex. I could say that the laws of physics on this pad were such that whenever anybody touched anyone else, their bodies fused; that the fusing was almost as painfully pleasurable as cumming; as squeezing an overripe pimple; and squeezing an overripe pimple whilst cumming; that neither I nor anyone said anything for some time, because neither I nor anyone existed; we were here, neither one nor many, neither alone nor together, and this was enough.

But none of this would explain why *enough* was so swiftly over. And why, when it was, my skin felt the way diet biscuits taste: like it was missing something.

'Is this some sort of post-identity utopia?' asked a voice that yes, I had to admit it, was mine.

'Only a cis white man would say that.'

'It's not a utopia, it's a fucking cushion.'

'A cushion for fucking on, yes, not talking shit.'

'Is this fabric biodegradable? I am pretty sure I can feel the microfibres grazing my liver.'

It was all starting to sound, feel, and indeed, smell, like that toilet queue.

'I've got a massive pimple on my back that I can feel but can't reach . . . will someone squeeze it?!'

'Eli!' I yelled.

'That's gross!'

'No kink-shaming in The Beyond.'

'No rules in The Beyond'.

'Pimple-picking is not a kink.'

'A kink can be anything.'

'Are we still on that date? Is this an elaborate story we've invented to escape the boredom of the queue? Have you wet yourself?'

'I'm not Eli.' A toe grazed my calf. 'And I thought dates died out like last decade.'

'Oh.'

'But you can still pick my pimple. If you want.'

'OK.'

As they directed my fingers towards the pimple, my cock bumped my thigh—if I'd been on a London tube train,

I'd take up four seats, *at least*—and the lily pad began to shake. I knew that if I let it go—if I could resist the desire to reach the limit of whatever this was—this world would remain. If I continued, however, it would end. It would end, and what followed might be worse. It might contain zero spaces for queers. Then again, it might be better. It might be beyond the structures that produced the feelings that necessitated words like 'better' and 'worse.' I'd like to say that it was whilst thinking of the latter that I did what I did, but it wasn't.

Reader, there was no *world* at that moment; there was just one big squeeze.

One big squeeze, and much sweating and panting, but nothing came out: not puss, not blood, not even water.

'Too early,' they sighed.

'No,' I said, 'it's too'—but the roof was all crack, and I was falling into it, and so I grabbed the lily pad, which was definitely *not* biodegradable, and would be here way longer than whichever human had dreamt it up.

Some People Have Real Problems

T HE PROBLEM WAS that the seesaw was so long it was impossible for whoever was at one end to see who was at the other; when they bounced too hard, or too fast, or too slow; when it seemed, for one terrible second, that they might fly right off and up into the sky before crashing down onto the ground, which was soggy and icy and cold, no matter how hot the sun burned in the sky, it was easy, too easy, to blame the other person, whom they could never see as a person in the way they saw themselves as a person, but as a vague weight for which everything was at fault.

The problem was that the seesaw was so short, it was impossible for whoever was at one end to see whoever was at the other as anything less than the thing that dominated their field of vision and determined when and how their body moved towards and away from the ground; when they bounced too hard, they bashed heads, sometimes lips, other times a non-visual feeling which, because the other words, the ones that would really describe whatever it was that wasn't happening, slipped off the seesaw's narrow body, they called love.

The problem was that the seesaw was not really a seesaw but was something its occupants, who clung to its slippery middle with their eyes shut and their mouths open, were too scared to see.

The problem was that the people on either end of it did not know how to picture their life as anything other than a problematic seesaw; they had no idea that there were places where people had never heard of either problems or seesaws, preferring, instead, to live amongst, for example, hammocks, ice-cream trucks, Post-it notes, and monkey bars.

Last Dance

THE PERCOLATOR BUBBLED at a frequency which made me certain the coffee would, this morning, be perfect. But as I reached for it, it toppled. I did not touch it; it toppled of its own accord. Then you came into the kitchen, surveyed the brown puddle now spreading across the hob and said: I thought you'd ordered a stand?

I said, Don't look at me like that.

You said, Like what.

I said, Like the world is ruined and it is all my fault.

You rolled your eyes. That is not what my look looked like.

How do you know? I said. You cannot look at your own look, well, only in the mirror, but then you are not looking at the same look that other people look at when they look at you.

By this point, you were looking at your phone. Bad leader had just said there was to be no more dancing, except in government-regulated spaces, which cost a hundred quid to enter. There was now very little part of the kitchen that was un-puddled.

Well, I said, *you* could've ordered the stand.

Yes, you said, but you *said* you'd done it.

I did do it!

Then why isn't it here?

I looked at my phone. Somebody's cat had adopted a flock of mice, even though mice don't live in flocks and cats don't have the legal capacity to adopt. Four different people had written books about mushrooms and how they would save us from everything. The percolator stand was still in my basket (along with a different kind of percolator and a pair of ugly but warm-looking slippers and a plastic avocado holder).

It's over, you said.

What? The word originated, not in my throat, but in the corner of the hob—the far corner—that was still un-puddled.

You waggled your hand in the direction of the puddle. This. You. Me. Us.

You're only saying what the guy said to the girl in that film we watched last night.

No, you said, we watched that the night before. Last night we went to Jo and Beryl's.

We don't know any Jo or any Beryl.

You looked me that look again. Then, you left.

The puddle has now dried into a brown stain that is shaped like that egg-shaped egg timer I bought from the back-of-the-lorry stalls at the back of the market, you know, the one you threw out because it didn't work, its idea of a minute was everyone else's idea of an hour and so everything ended up flubbery and overdone, at least, those were the words you used; to me, all that erroneous time only enriched the flavour. One day, I'll have seen all there is to see in it; on this day, I will unwrap the plastic casing of the special coffee-stain-removal cloth I bought from the same website from which I did not quite buy the percolator stand; the kitchen will be clean again, and if things are still happening that I wish wouldn't happen, I will, at least, be able to explain them. I may even do a small, illegal dance. But that day has not come—yet.

After The Noise

IT'S THAT TIME—AGAIN.

    'Come *on*. I don't want No.18 reporting us for being late.' Leah shoves my arms into my coat as if I'm her toddler.

    It's Thursday, it's 8.00 p.m., it's the Two Minute Scream. It's   *[whilst participation is not mandatory, numerous studies have shown]*

              but I don't want
                    to do it.

    What I want   is to know what life was like before the Cha *[there is no evidence to suggest]* and whether *[cortisol levels were]*

    'Let's stay in and fuck?'

    What I want   is her nipples in my *[there is no]* mouth.

    'Let's dust off that purple cock we only tried once?'

    'What? Hurry *up*.'

    Whenever I want what the Channel does not want me *[participation is not mandatory but]* to want—and especially when something is about to happen that it wants me to want to happen—it gets the sort of loud that gets   *[higher in the control group]* in *[significantly]*   your bones.

It gets the sort of loud that scrapes its nails against
[there is no evidence to]   the chalkboards you d i d n ' t
know   were in your bones   *[participation is not]*

because chalkboards   do not exist in the sorts of
[there is no] bones that exist on the   *[mandatory but]*
Science Channel.

It gets the sort of loud that gets your feet into your shoes
and the whole of you into the carpark outside of your flat
[boa constrictor, probably illegal]   without you knowing
      how

            it happened

                        or—

aaaaaaaaaaaaaarrrrrrrrrrggggggggggggghhhhh-
hhhhhhaaaaaaaarrrrrrrrrrggggggggghhhhhhhhhh-
hhhaaaaaaaaaaaaaarrrrrrrrrrggggggggggggghhhhh-
hhhhhhaaaaaaaarrrrrrrrrrggggggggghhhhhhhhhh-
hhhaaaaaaaaaaaaaarrrrrrrrrrgggggggggggggghhhhh-
hhhhhhaaaaaaaarrrrrrrrrrggggggggghhhhhhhhhh-
hhhaaaaaaaaaaaaaarrrrrrrrrrggggggggggggghhhhh-
hhhhhhaaaaaaaarrrrrrrrrrggggggggghhhhhhhhhh-
hhhaaaaaaaaaaaaaarrrrrrrrrrgggggggggggggghhhhh-
hhhhhhaaaaaaaarrrrrrrrrrggggggggghhhhhhhhhh-
hhhaaaaaaaaaaaaaarrrrrrrrrrgggggggggggggghhhhh-
hhhhhhaaaaaaaarrrrrrrrrrggggggggghhhhhhhhhh-
hhhaaaaaaaaaaaaaarrrrrrrrrrgggggggggggggghhhhh-
hhhhhhhaaaaaaaarrrrrrrrrrggggggggghhhhhhhhhh-
hhhaaaaaaaaaaaaaarrrrrrrrrrggggggggggggggghhhhh-
hhhhhhhaaaaaaaarrrrrrrrrrggggggggghhhhhhhhhhhh-
haaaaaaaaaaaaaarrrrrrrrrrgggggggggggggghhhhhhhhhh-

haaaaaaarrrrrrrrrggggggggghhhhhhh*aaaaaaaaaaaarrrrrr-
rrrrggggggggggggghhhhhhhhhhhaaaaaaarrrrrrrrrggggggggh-
hhhhhhhhhh*

—After the scream comes the rainbow, and after everyone
uploads the rainbow to their LookAtWhatI'veJustLooke-
dAt Channel come the Speeches.

From No.42: *I scream to remember my husband, whose
liver packed in on the second day of the Noise.* The event of
her husband's death is sewn so thoroughly into her face—
particularly in the skin around the eyes—that everyone
claps and sighs as if hearing this story for the first time.

The thought comes that there must be other ways to
live than this, but before I can do anything with it, No.13
pipes up: *I scream to remember the first day of the Filters.
Anyone else?* He pauses, stops, points at me. *You, do you
remember?* I try to indicate that I wasn't raising my hand; I
was simply scratching my nose. *Thought not,* he continues,
clucking as if to award himself a point in whatever game
he thinks life is. *My Noise had been taunting me all night,
it took the form of millions and billions of tiny stick figures,
half-human, half-ant, scuttling constantly over the inside and
the outside of my brain. I am—I'm—I am a strong man.
Brave and true. But it was wearing me down. It was. And I'm
not sure. I'm not sure if I would be here today, were it not for
that morning when I awoke—not to peace, no, but something
better. In place of those dastardly ant-people was the Channel.
Except, I did not know, at that early point, what it was. What
I knew was that it was, it was—it was as if my brain had been
replaced by a spreadsheet, and whilst I am not in the habit of
adoring spreadsheets, I have to admit that this one, the way it*

fluttered, inside my head, but also, somehow, outside of it—it was sublime. *Yes. Yes, my entry into the world in which we are currently fortunate enough to find ourselves was so sublime that I, a brave strong man, as I may have already mentioned, well, I did—I did cry.*

When his speech is finally over—though whether the words are his own or a parrot of the History Channel, no one knows—my feet are the same temperature and texture as the tarmac, my mug of tea is pushing at my bladder's seams, the Channels are pushing at my brain's seams, and all of these facts are pushing at the seams of my face, and I wish they would burst but they won't, they never do, everything just stays the same. No. 28, 35 and 49 are crying; no.75 is telling anyone who will listen that the Channel is less a spreadsheet than a singer who also happens to know everything about everything . And Leah—Leah is staring at me as if the only thing wrong with this scene is me.

We have three friends: Hen, Illy and Reva. When we are with them, Leah holds my hand so tight that it is coated with her sweat. She sits not so much next to as on top of me, and Hen thinks we're—'not the *perfect* couple. Obviously there is no such thing as the perfect couple, but you two are the sort that makes people hope there *might* be.'

Illy says we are the only couple they know who has been together since the Beginning of the End of the Noise.

'No,' says Reva, 'there's also Adam and Ev.'

'Adam and Ev!' says Hen. 'You couldn't make it up.'

'Actually, you could,' says Illy. 'And I think they did. I don't think they were really together before the Noise; I think they just like to think that because —'

'—*All unhappy queers are alike; all happy queers are happy in their own way. Discuss.*' Leah is parroting the Love Languages Channel: LGBT edition, which in itself is parroting some book from the backend of the Before, but she grins as if she came up with it herself.

'I've never seen a couple that's happy the way you two are, that's for sure!' says Reva.

'*Oh stop,*' says Leah, batting her eyelids in the manner of a drag queen who is being told exactly what she wants to hear.

When we are with our friends, their words stiffen my upper-lip hair into a moustache I hope will never grow out.

It does though, the moustache. It always does.

We are with our friends no more than once a fortnight and when we are not with them, Leah acts as if she is, say, the dining table, and I, say, that grubby little bathroom cabinet whose toothpaste stains she constantly blames me for a) creating and b) never wiping off. We are with our friends no more than once a fortnight because whenever I suggest we see them more often, she says, 'Sometimes I think you prefer hanging out with them than with me.'

'No—'

       [goats climbing on top of other goats so as to munch] —'I just —'   *[Unregulated weath]*
   [Anxious]   *[Now might be a good moment to reflect on]*
     [What is your]
[Depression isn't feeling]   *[er]*
  [?]   *[Fresh or frozen?]*
 [What is your]   *[Don't take things for]* *[Dungarees]*

[Attachment Style]

We were all alive in the Before the Noise but we can't remember it. We can watch films from it, we can read books from it, we can listen to records from it, except that the Channels are always between us and it, just as they are between us and sleep, us and the thoughts that might *[let go of what]* between us and *[your free subscription to the LGBT Relationship Coaching Gold is about to expire!]* us.

We were all alive in the Before the Noise but we can't remember it because Evolution. Because *[let go of what does not serve you]*. Because *[we are living in a time of unprecedented]* Because *[if you are the type to throw yourself a pity party over a disappointing avocado, just imagine what]* Because zero-waste consciousness: *[the average person of the before wasted 2.6 trillion tonnes of space-time a day, not including sleep!]* Because—well, it depends on the Channel.

'I just find it callous.' Leah is referring to my failure to express any emotion besides irritation, even through this week's post-scream speeches.

'They're all the same.'

'But No.25 lost all of her children and No.19 accidentally strangled his cat due to an auto-immune response to the Noise that he is still dealing with. I mean, not to be rude, but did you see that rash on his face?'

'It's not the words that are the same but the feelings underneath them. Like they've been over-polished.'

She wrinkles her nose. 'You can't polish feelings.'

'And don't you think it's suspicious that the speeches always feature a loss for which no one and nothing besides the Noise is responsible, and that the end is almost a variation on theme of "Then the Channels came and saved me"? Don't you think it's a bit too obvious that, like the rainbow, they want us to believe that the way we're living now is the only and the correct way?'

Her face is blotchy with pain. 'You act like the Noise was no big deal when it killed so many people. When it's still killing people. When *some* of us are still trying —.'

I parrot the Silly Animal Facts Channel:*[when parrots are sexually frustrated, they masturbate on inanimate objects]*'

She makes her 'not funny' eyes at me, then: '*[Silliness is a defence against trauma and a dangerous one]*'

—*['when female parrots go longer than three weeks without sex, they lose control of their faculties']*

—'*[85% of relationships where one partner refuses to share their Noise Story end prematurely]*'

—'OK, *OK*, I'll tell you what happened. I'll tell you what I saw. Felt. Heard. Whatever.' I close my eyes. I close my eyes because closing the eyes is a thing faces do when they want to show other faces that they are encountering some sort of Deep. 'The wind was loud, very very loud, but it was loud in a way that was beautiful. So beautiful it hurt. As in, it cut me. It was like receiving continual paper cuts all over my body.' A tear rolls down my left cheek. 'I was with my mum and when she saw what it was doing to me, she, well, soon after that, she died.'

My words are one part a flailing towards my memories of what other people have told me about what they tell themselves about what they experienced in the Noise, two parts something else. What this 'else' is and whether it comes from inside or outside of me, I do not know.

'Babe.'

In the room: me, her, the sofa I am sitting on, the table, the chair she is sitting on, the chair she is not sitting on, the TV, the box of random crap neither of us could ever sit on, and our Channels, which are nowhere, which is everywhere.

'Don't you feel relieved?' Now she is sitting not so much next to as on top of me.

I say the nothing that I feel.

'You know, now that you've opened up?'

I nod.

It's not that I've lied; it's that I've invented the third person—the one whose gaze convinces her that girlfriends is what we are. Then she runs into the bedroom and already I know that she'll return with the purple cock.

Everyone remembers the Noise differently, but what I don't know is whether anyone besides me fails to remember it at all. I do not remember if it felt like snails sliming over my body (what Hen told me twice whilst high), or if it sounded like the wailing of the world's most difficult baby were that baby trapped in the engine of a steam train (what Hen told me once whilst almost sober). I do not remember if it made me think I could do headstands when I could not actually do headstands, and although it was immediately apparent that I could not do headstands, I nevertheless kept trying to do headstands in the belief this was the only way to stop it, and which resulted, instead, in longterm brain damage (Neil P on the Other People's Pain Channel).

I do not remember who or what it took from me. I do not remember if it took anything from me. I do not remember what I told Leah I remembered. I do not know how, when she follows all the advice of the Positive Recovery Channel—*write down one gain for every loss, and if you can't think of one, make one!*—she can be so sure.

'Why don't you have a go?' she says. 'It's really helped me. I used to feel so bitter and angry that I'd lost both of my parents when other people had theirs, but then I spent a day reflecting on the Toxic Relationships: Parental Edition Channel, and it made me realise that everyone suffers in their own way, it's not a competition, and that I have a lot to be grateful for, such as a job which pays for a gold membership to all the health and mental health channels, a job I love, a flat I like, and a partner I love, too.'

'I guess I'm sad that I lost my friends—'

'You lost your friends?' she interrupts. 'You didn't tell me that.'

It's just a feeling, a lump, a breeze, which is never reported on the Weather (or any other) Channel, but she wants a story, and I want to give her what she wants, and I know how to do it, and I do. I furnish it with names and mannerisms, with moments of tension, climax and release, after which, what is lost can never be recovered, and what is gained can never be spoken, and she is crying, and I am pretending to cry, and she is squeezing my hand and saying how close she feels to me, how sorry she is that she sometimes takes me for granted, takes us for granted: 'I mean, have you listened to any of the Lost Loves of the Noise Channel? Heart-breaking.'

But there's a chemical tartness in my throat like I've swallowed something I'm not supposed to swallow, like washing-up liquid, or shoe polish.

My earliest memory? Waking up with my nose pressed against Leah's neck, my Silly Channel tickling the edges of my throat, and a rumbling between the mattress and the walls like I was in the belly of something too big and too hungry to be heard.

But there is another thing that happens in my body. It is not remembering. It is not any sort of -ing that leads to
[11 Signs of Self-Sabotage]
[what is the future of]
[129 more crisp packets have been recycled from your street this week than] *[productivity has increased by 87% since the introduction of Working Week Weather]*
a *[For example, bone health]*

story

The other thing that happens   happens in the space where my appendix used to be. My not-appendix. What happens is that it misses the silence. It misses the silence from the time Before the Noise. It does not remember this time and yet it misses the silence the most. Of this and only this am I sure—maybe.

Either Happy, So Happy, Too Happy Or

A T LAST, THE sun was shining, the bloke next door had stopped drilling his man cave or his sex dungeon or whatever, and there was a buzz in your chest like you'd swallowed the £192-worth of electricity the power company insisted it was correct to charge you for the month of August, even though you'd sent them screenshots and photos to prove that you'd spent that month in France, and although you knew this was just one example of the OTT metaphorical thinking to which Happy You was prone, it made you feel as if you could do anything. The question was: what?

Calling up the electricity company might be a good place to start; sure, they'd put you on hold, but you could scrub the kitchen floor whilst you waited, and the hold music might, if you got lucky, be a pop song you'd never admit you liked, well, apart from to the person in your head to whom you were always talking, but they didn't count, they were probably just a part of yourself you'd not discover until your forties or whatever, although thirty-two wasn't that far from forty, it was a lot closer than twenty-nine, and twenty-nine is what you often said when people asked your age, but what did any of this matter? And how is it that, of all the things you could be doing, you were just standing on a sticky patch of what you now remembered was peach beer, your fingers opening and closing as if expecting to grasp, amongst the flat's stale air, something solid?

SAD, SO SAD, TOO SAD

At last, the sun was shining, the bloke next door had stopped drilling his man cave or his sex dungeon or whatever, but the hole in your chest, which you knew was just one example of the OTT metaphorical thinking to which Sad You was prone—and to which you had, in many WhatsApp messages, attributed to the absence of the sun and the presence of the drilling—was still there.
Things! Could you do them?

No, you could not.

All night, you'd not slept; now it was almost midday and you had a deadline at five and a Teams meeting at three, and when you'd logged into your email this morning, you'd found yet another version of that message from your boss where she almost suggested you couldn't be trusted to work from home, but still—you could not get up.

You could, however, message your boss to the effect that you'd switched off her Outlook notifications so as to concentrate on perfecting the document for this afternoon's deadline, and the boss replied with the sweaty-foreheaded smiley, at which point you noticed that there was so much sweat on your own forehead, several strands of hair were stuck to it, but you could not unstick them; you couldn't do anything, although, it had to be admitted, you had now been not-doing it for so long that it was starting to feel a lot like *something*, and it was only with the aim of putting off, yet again, the moment of finding out what it was, that you got up.

After staring at the dishcloth in the kitchen sink for more time than you'd care to measure, lifting your laptop from your bed to your table was somehow possible, as was logging into Teams. Allow App access to your camera? No. *My connection's still dodgy soz.* As noise began to spill out of the holes in the faces on the screen—your hole was somewhat of a narcissist, and saw its ugly un-self in absolutely everything—you noticed the stain on the floorboards. It was orange, and looking at it made you rub your eyes to make sure you'd not suddenly developed conjunctivitis. Sounds were still coming out of the screen holes, and you grabbed the dishcloth, whose mustiness was more refreshing than you'd expected. Only as you wiped off the last of the stain did you remember its birth: your friend had spilt her fancy peach beer, then apologised, vigorously, repeatedly, as if she'd done something *truly* heinous; she'd wanted to clear it up but you'd grabbed her hand and told her that worse things had happened at sea and she'd said yes but the sea isn't sticky and you'd said let's check on the aubergine, you tried to say it as if there was no part of you that wanted to kiss her excema-wrinkled fingers before you let them go, and now a voice that was almost certainly outside of your head was asking what you thought about the proposal? You wiped your forehead only to find it dry and hairless, and for some reason this filled you with a thing that made turning on your camera possible.

You opened your mouth and things fell out, and the holes in the faces opened and closed and opened and closed, and although you knew they represented people with worries and fears and fantasies and hopes and dreams and inexplicable crushes of their own, all you saw was that gif that peach-friend sometimes sent you, apropros of nothing, of starving baby birds.

Then the meeting was over, and there was still forty-five minutes until the deadline, but you emailed your manager—as if to suggest that the person who'd finished the document three days early whilst on hold to the electricity company who'd charged you for power you'd never used, was still you.

AND FOR NO GOOD REASON

'But what if it's both?' was the first thing your friend said when you told her you didn't know which version was true. 'Or couldn't the truth be somewhere in between, or scattered everywhere, like ashes? Or what if the truth is a kind of sea where better things actually happen haha?' She squeezed your hand, her tone just like that of the man at the energy company who'd insisted that if the meter said you'd spent £192-worth of energy then you must've spent £192-worth of energy, and if you didn't know how, then what about a spare key, what about friends who abused your trust to lie around all day with the heating on, having sex parties and growing weed, and when you'd laughed, he'd said, it may sound far-fetched, but it happened more than you'd think, and, 'Life,' your friend was saying, 'is more about what you don't know than what you do,' and as you'd opened your mouth to say that although you had plenty of friends, not one had a spare key, he'd hung up, and then you said that you hated how she said this as if she had a detailed spreadsheet of all the unknowns specific to you, and then you watched her fingers dangle in the air, which was somehow fresher than it had been, though it was a long time, probably too long, since you'd opened a window.

Who's There?

I N MY HEAD, a knocking. The gaps between each knock were such that you could tell the knocker was pissed off. I was good at telling such things because I grew up in a house where the doorbell was always about to be fixed. But bodies are not houses and the only person inside mine was me, and so I sautéd onions, and I set a phone reminder to hang up the washing as soon as it was done, and I checked in on my friends who liked to be checked in on, and I told my boyfriend that I'd fuck him as soon as I'd finished reading this page—and you would think that all these verbs would knock the knocking (knocker?) away from the door of me, but it did not.

My boyfriend fell asleep as soon as he came. Not wanting to watch the cum dry to his leg hairs, I rolled over. I picked up my book, but the knocker was pushing the letters out of its words, its words off its pages; I dropped it on the carpet. I picked it up, then dropped it again—hard. I wanted it to wake my boyfriend up, but his breathing deepened; his body was doing all the miraculous REM healing whilst I—I was still being plagued by this mystery knocker.

I dashed to the bathroom, hoping, at last, to confront him. But in the mirror, I did not see the huge, hairy fist I'd expected. I did not see any of my childhood friends' mothers, their foreheads wrinkled and rain-damp. I did not see Jim, my very first boyfriend, crying because he thought I'd stood him up. But I didn't see a thirty-year-old woman, either. First, I saw the breasts: they'd been stuck on, clumsily, by a toddler, or someone who'd made them whilst also, for example, watching a TV show about a well-to-do family who become drug pushers, whilst cross-stitching. The face wasn't mine, either; there was another face inside it. It wanted to get out and I wanted to help it, but when I lunged at the glass, it disappeared. There was a big red spot by my eyebrow; I squeezed it, but it wasn't ready, and although I knew it wasn't ready, I kept squeezing it, I thought it might coax the knocker out, but no; all that came was blood, and so much, that the next morning, my manager pulled me to one side and asked if everything was OK at home.

'Yes,' I said, then began to cry.

'Your boyfriend seems very nice,' she said, 'but you never know.'

I could not say about the knocker, nor about how I'd been desperate for him to leave, yet now that he had, I felt like the loneliest person in the world, which is a feeling I thought I'd left in the house with the broken bell.

My stomach ached. 'I'm about to get my period.'

She sighed like she was disappointed that I was not, in fact, a victim of sexual violence, but only of the tragedy that was the body from which neither she nor anyone could save me. 'OK, umm, well, maybe take some codeine or something? I mean, I want to kill everyone for like ten days before mine, which has actually been for the last ten days, but you'd never have guessed, would you?'

'Actually,' I said, 'when you pressed that slice of coffee cake into my hand after I said that I didn't like coffee cake, and said, just try it, it's delicious, not daring to admit that you just wanted me to stay late to finish that project you'd guilt-tripped me into working on, I felt like you *did* want kill me.'

She looked at her feet, then at me, then back at her feet. 'Maybe you should see your doctor.'

I spent the rest of that day going over and over that moment, but I still couldn't tell who'd said those words— me, or the knocker.

When I told my boyfriend about the conversation with my manager, he did not laugh, as I'd expected; he made a face which suggested that were he living in a universe maybe three permutations away from this one, he'd be crying. 'You've really got to stop picking your spots. You probably wouldn't have them anymore if you didn't pick them.'

I didn't tell him that I'd got way more since exiting my twenties; my body was trying, fruitlessly, to travel backwards in time.

We hadn't bothered to buy any curtains, and, behind him, I saw my reflection in the darkened window, only, it wasn't mine. It was a boy's. Jim's? No. I'd not seen him before. I squinted. Again, he was gone.

'I just hate the idea of people thinking I could hurt you.'

'But she didn't, that's the point.'

'But what if I did?' He looked at his hands, which

were huge; they could crush me if they wanted, which they didn't, but still.

I laced my fingers between his. 'You won't.'

He nodded.

I lurched towards him.

He pulled away. 'What?'

I thought I'd seen a girl flit across his face, but no, I was just tired and PMSing, he was the manliest man that ever did stomp across this earth. 'Just saw a pimple I wanted to pick, is all.'

'You're terrible.'

We both laughed.

'I know.'

The next morning, I woke with blood-soaked pjs, but I saw the boy, there, in the blood, or maybe in my hurry to soak it out of the flannel, I'm not sure, but he was in me, I'd let him in, only I didn't know when I'd opened the door. Or maybe he could make himself small enough to squeeze through letterboxes, or ears, or mouths; or maybe someone who wasn't me had let him in, the way my mum used to let my friends in without telling me and then I'd come downstairs to find her talking at them, the way she used to talk at me, and I'd think, what, are they *her* kids now, but no; my mum now lived in a flat with an incredibly loud buzzer which was, more to the point, over two-hundred miles away, and a person couldn't have more than one other person living inside them, surely. I put on a skirt and tights, but they felt wrong in the way my breasts felt wrong, so I kicked them off. I pulled on my boyfriend's jeans. They were too big, but something about their too-bigness felt just right.

'What are you doing?' He looked exceedingly sorry for himself, as if waking up was qualitatively harder for him than for anyone else.

'Nothing.' As soon as I let go of the waistband, the jeans dropped to my ankles.

'You look hilarious.'

'Thanks.' My hairs prickled as I pulled the tights back on.

'Much better,' he said, staring at the boobs that were no longer mine, just as I/the boy, was sure that Rick's pecks were really his.

'You look . . . *gay*,' was the first thing Rick said when I cut my hair shorter than his.

'Well, I *am* bi.'

I'd told him this many times, but he made the face he made when he'd thought he was about to win a board game, but, owing to some last-minute trick of fate, lost. 'Oh yes.'

'I think . . . I need to explore it.'

'You mean, you want to break up?'

We'd been together since we were eighteen; imagining my life without him was like imagining my body without a head. 'No.'

He exhaled. 'OK.'

'You can explore, too.'

'I'm not attracted to guys.'

'I mean, with girls.'

'Oh.' He made a face I'd never seen before. 'OK.'

There was so much to say that I said nothing. Then he asked if I wanted to watch an episode of *Madmen*. I nodded.

Three episodes later, I'd just about fallen asleep, when he shimmied over to my side of the bed and squeezed my boob. I didn't want to fuck, but I knew that if I communicated this, he'd think it was because of what we'd sort of discussed before, so I rolled over and made the sort of noises I'd make if I did want to. Then I closed my eyes and imagined the sorts of things I usually imagined to make me cum: things involving women. That night, however, it didn't work. So, for the first time in all the time we'd been together, I faked it.

'Wow, that seemed like a really big one,' he said, kissing my back.

'Yeah,' I lied, fixing my eye on a sock that had been on the floor for so long, its icing of dust was thicker than it.

'Mind if I try from behind?'

I didn't like it from behind, but I said, sure. He slid out, then back into me, squeezing my buttocks. It hurt, but not in a bad way. I closed my eyes.

You're a boy.

I opened my eyes. The voice was neither mine nor Rick's, but if we were the only people in the room, whose was it? I supposed it was the boy's, but it didn't sound like him, quite. I closed my eyes.

Just two boys fucking.

Now, I was wet. I was a boy being fucked by a boy and as I/he was about to cum, Rick did.

'That felt even better than usual,' he said.

I hoped the voice might interject, telling me what to feel, or, at least, say. But it didn't, and so I just nodded, fighting the sudden compulsion to lick the dust off that sock.

At work, the first person to see my hair was the new receptionist, who called me sir. I smiled. She blushed. 'Sorry,' she said, 'I mean, erm, madame.' I wanted to tell her not to worry; that whilst I disliked the word 'sir' almost as much as the word 'madame,' her mistake felt somehow right. But of course, you can't go around saying things like that, especially not at work, and then my manager walked in. I could tell, from her face, that she hated it. 'It's very, um, *short*,' she said, eventually.

Other things people said about my hair: 'cute' and 'what will you do with your hairbands' and 'short,' and when I joked that they probably meant I looked like a lesbian, they said no, no no no, certainly not, as if that would be truly *terrible*. In supermarkets, I got ID'd twice as often. I got a few more sirs, a few suspicious stares in public toilets; in other places, I got stares that tried to hide their suspiciousness under a frenetic looking away-then-towards. Once, some teenagers chased me across a park, demanding to know if I was a boy or a girl. 'I'm not being rude,' said what looked like a boy. 'I just want to know.' I should've thanked him for daring to ask what no one else did, not even myself. Instead, I said it was none of his business, then stalked off.

I was a woman, but the boy, having spent so long hidden under layers of stretchy nylon and badly-applied eyeshadow, was still a teenager. Now unleashed, he was doing a lot of teenage-boy things, like not talking to people if he didn't feel like talking to them, eating whatever he wanted, not doing things if he didn't feel like doing them, even if he was being paid to do them, and drugs. He/I/we, did a lot of drugs. I did them with mostly straight women, in clubs, whilst Rick was either playing video games with his friends, or asleep. Every now and then, I'd lock eyes across the dance floor with a woman. She'd smile at the me that was neither man nor woman, girl nor boy, but some combination of the above for which there was no word. Sometimes we'd dance, occasionally, we'd kiss, and when we did, I'd feel, for a moment, that I was spinning off the gender axis, but mostly she'd start chewing her lips and grinning at some boy in a sweaty white t-shirt, and I'd remember we were just really, really high.

Rick, however, only saw the girl. He saw the weight that the boy's food habits had put on my hips and bum and boobs and said: 'hot.' The tighter, the more girlish clothes I wore, the more often he said it. When I wore loose, boyish clothes, he didn't look at me, let alone touch me, and even if he did, he was only touching the girl parts of me, which weren't really mine. But when people asked how our open relationship was going, I said *awesome;* I said, he's so sweet so supportive, but the looks on people's faces told me I was losing my womanly ability to make everyone feel like everything was alright.

When I was late for work three days in a row, my boss gave me another Talk. 'I know this isn't Sampson and Delila but erm you have sort of changed since you cut your hair. You're making lots of mistakes, and if people point it out, you don't seem to care, and the other day, when I started to tell you how intermittent fasting was really sharpening up my thoughts, you just walked away, and Mandy said you did the same thing about her holiday, it's rude, and it's bad for morale, and you didn't even apologise for not meeting your last deadline . . . It's like you don't want to be here.'

I tried to remember what it was she was paying me for; I failed. 'I don't.'

'What?'

'I quit.' I was smiling. The boy was smiling. Only when we saw Rick's face that evening, over dinner, did we stop. 'But what will you do for money? What about the mortgage?'

You are a woman.

He was right. I pushed my plate away. 'You're right.'

You are still a woman. With a man. With a mortgage. With a mortgage you share with a man.

'Don't you want that?' He nodded at my plate.

I shook my head.

'Please don't start that again.'

'What?'

'The not-eating. You've been so much better with it since you, you know . . .'

'I know,' I said. I remembered how, when my body had looked and acted more like a boy's body—flat-chested; periodless—it hadn't felt like one; nor had it felt like a girl's, and certainly not like a woman's; it felt like nothing because I'd starved the part that dictated the opening and the closing of the doors through which my genders came and went into something like death. 'I'm just a bit stressed.' I forced down some more pasta.

I spent my remaining time at work applying for other jobs, composing not-too-desperate-sounding freelance requests, and looking forward to whatever combination of boy and girl would emerge from whatever combination of powders, techno and sweat I imbibed that weekend.

Only, it didn't work anymore. The music was great, the drugs were great, but I felt . . . I felt like I'd queued and queued for a water slide only to find, in place of the slide, a hole. It was too deep to see to the bottom and yet I knew there was something terrible there. I wanted to turn back but there was no back to turn to, only sweaty, gurning, people, so I jumped.

'You're cute.'

I landed in the voice of a woman. She grabbed me by the waist, then spun me around. I tripped over a foot, though I couldn't tell if it was mine or hers. She laughed. Then she whispered something in my ear. Too loud to hear what she said, but I smiled and nodded as if I had. We danced and kissed and she slid her hands up under my shirt and then the music stopped and the lights came on and she said, 'This doesn't have to be over because the music is over do you want to come back to mine?'

I stamped the ground. It was solid. Had her voice tugged me back up to the top of the hole, or had our dancing been a long, slow falling, and this, the bottom? I nodded.

Just as I was lying on her mattress, about to cum—the knocking.

Fuck's sake, I said, or maybe it was the boy, who is it and what do you want?

No reply.

Her tongue was all over my clit and my clit was a clit was a cock and—oh—wow—I pushed her head away. 'Thanks.'

'Already?' She wiped her mouth. 'Like a boy.'

'Sorry.'

'Don't be. My girlfriend takes so long, I sometimes invent new words to amuse myself.'

'You've got a girlfriend?'

She ran her finger from my belly button to my hip, and it didn't look like a boy's, it didn't look like a girl's, and what it did or didn't look like had nothing to do with how much fat it did or didn't have; it just was. 'We're open.'

'So are me and my boyfriend.'

She screamed. 'No way have you got a *boyfriend*.' She spat out the word like she wanted it inside her for as little time as possible—exactly how I'd always wanted to say it. 'Shit. Sorry. It's just you're so—'

'I know.'

We talked for a few more hours, at the end of which time she began to annoy me, and when we swapped numbers on her doorstep a few hours later, I knew that we both knew that we were only doing so to avoid admitting that we didn't want to see each other again.

When I got home, Rick was shooting CGI zombies. I didn't realise I was standing in front of the screen until he shouted at me. 'I've been stuck on that level for ages.'

'Sorry.'

'What do you want?'

I did not know that in eight months' time, I'd sit where he was now sitting, telling my newish girlfriend—who wasn't really a girlfriend because they was nonbinary but there is no good word for nonbinary friend—that I didn't know why it had taken me so long to work out that I wanted to break up; but I knew that the 'you' to whom he was speaking could never be me.

'What do I want? What do I want?'

In my head, a knocking. Come in, I said, please, come in, and tell me something profound. But the voice that said, eggs, said, sausages, said, hash browns, sounded exactly the way my voice would sound had it been up all night talking to strangers and snorting drugs.

'Brunch,' I said.

'Sure.' He glanced at the screen. 'But can I just have one more game?'

Then I chopped mushrooms and he carried on killing creatures that were already dead.

Inappropriate

THE BEST THING about your cock was that no one could see it, not even if you wore leggings. When you sat on the bus, backpack on lap, hands on backpack, what people saw was a woman who expected to be robbed. If they noticed you were clutching the backpack so tightly that all the tendons in your hands were sticking out, they might wonder whether they were the one that she, the woman you were not, was afraid of. They'd never guess that under the cotton and Lycra and canvas made from eight and a half recycled plastic bottles, you were hard. You hadn't cum this way—yet. But you were only twenty-six; there was time.

There was, however, more and more time where 'best' felt like 'worst,' e.g. when people called you girl or sweetheart or luv or darling or lady e.g. when one of the cismen you still sometimes made the mistake of getting off with squeezed your tits whilst ramming their cocks too deep into your vagina and even when they'd stopped they'd look at you as if tits and vagina were all that you were e.g. when you'd finally found a pair of loose jeans in which your cock could swing freely, only to catch, in the shop window—you avoided mirrors—the half-reflection of what looked, yes, you had to admit it, a lot like a woman.

What there was not yet enough of were the times when a queer looked at you like they *knew*.

What few there were never occurred on the very rare Tinder dates who were neither a) your exes nor b) your exes' exes nor c) your friends nor d) your friends' exes, but always with some rando in some place wildly inappropriate, e.g. that coffee/bakery/plant/gift shop that had just opened in what used to be a public toilet and was, unsurprisingly, cramped.

As you reached for your flat white, Milly launched into her third and, you hoped, final description of her flatmate's refusal to believe that his pet snake insisted on slithering around her ankles whilst she boiled the kettle each morning, and you knocked elbows with what was not so much a woman with an undercut as an undercut with a woman. She looked you *the* look and you looked it back and she smiled and the cock whispered at you to whisper, *Let's go back to mine and fuck*, but you ignored it, you had to, not even the man you weren't would get away with saying such things, except, perhaps, were he there for the cottaging that must've taken place on the coffee shop's retro metro tiles, unless they were new metro tiles simply designed to imply deviancy whilst keeping it at a safe distance, which could easily be what was happening with this undercut, there was no law against straight people having them, though there should be, and now the woman was rubbing the leaf of a spider plant and cooing as if it was a baby, and you could suddenly imagine her boyfriend going at her with the clippers that morning whilst she did his manbun and—'Do you know her?'

Now Milly was looking at you as if you were as terrible as her flatmate's pet snake, and you wished so much that she'd stop that you said, 'Isn't this coffee delicious,' though you'd not yet tasted it.

'Yes, way better than last week's,' said Milly, and you wondered why hiding the truth of your body was so easy yet hard, and why your crotch was now tingling as if you hadn't already wondered this many, many, too many, times, before.

Acknowledgements

T HANK YOU TO early reader, Lucy Caldwell, for excellent advice and encouragement.

Thanks to magazines and journals to published some of the stories that make up this collection: *A Queer Anthology of Wilderness*, *Prototype*, *Short Fiction*, *Minor Lits*, *3:am*, *Hobart Pulp*, *Entropy*, and *The London Magazine*.

Thanks to my PhD supervisors, Alice and Campbell, for intellectual and moral support over the writing of these stories.

Thanks to all my friends and family for the care, support, laughter, pizza, deep chats, silly chats, and lots more. Thanks in particular to Sarah for the writing chats.

Thank you Nicky for all the love and stickers.

Thank you Chris and Jen for taking a punt on my strange collection.

This book has been typeset by
SALT PUBLISHING LIMITED
using Granjon, a font designed by George W. Jones
for the British branch of the Linotype company in the
United Kingdom. It is manufactured using Holmen
Bulky News 52gsm, a Forest Stewardship Council™
certified paper from the Hallsta Paper Mill in Sweden.
It was printed and bound by Clays Limited in Bungay,
Suffolk, Great Britain.

CROMER
GREAT BRITAIN
MMXXIII